THE ALIEN'S RETURN

GRACE KENSINGTON

1

———

Eden could still feel Loralia shaking beside her as they stepped out of the lab and into the dim hallway. She couldn't imagine what the delicate, beautiful woman was feeling as she tried to process what she had just learned. All her life Loralia had believed that one man had been her father and that he had died along with the others of her kind during the mysterious plague that destroyed all but her in their underground realm. Only moments before, however, she had been confronted by another man who proclaimed himself to be her father. Though she had recently learned that she was not of pure Irisa blood and that she was, indeed, part Eteri, Eden could see in her eyes that she had not fully considered that that meant the man she had always considered her father, the man who she loved and who had taught her how to utilize the tremendous power that her Irisa heritage had given her, was not the man who had truly sired her.

"Loralia?"

The sound of the unfamiliar voice from behind them made Eden stop. She felt Loralia stiffen in her arms and saw the woman's lavender eyes close as if she were trying to block out the presence of the man by pretending that he wasn't there.

"Please," the voice said.

It was low and grainy in a strange, intangible way as if the man who was speaking hadn't used the voice in quite some time and was just now getting accustomed to forming words again.

"Loralia," Eden said softly. "Do you want to see him?"

Loralia stayed still and silent for a few seconds. Eden didn't rush her. She wanted to give her as much time as she needed to work through what was happening around her. A moment later, though, Loralia surprised her by turning suddenly and facing the man who was coming up behind her. Towering nearly as large as the Denynso warriors and bearing tattered wings that hung by his sides, the man was something that Eden had never seen. He was startling in an uncomfortable, out-of-balance way that was unlike anything that Eden had ever experienced. Even when she had first encountered the Denynso warriors, she had not felt this sense of discomfort. She didn't know if she could truly describe the feeling as fear, but it was something unnerving that put her on edge. As she met his eyes, however, she saw something deep within them that pled for calm and sought understanding.

"Who are you?" Loralia asked. "Who *are* you?"

"My name is Azrael," he said. "I'm your father."

"No," she said, shaking her head. "No. You're not my father."

Azrael nodded and took another step toward her. Loralia held her ground, straightening her shoulders and facing down the man in a way that somehow made him stop and look at her beseechingly.

"Please."

Eden felt a hand close around her arm and looked up to see Pyra standing beside her.

"We need to keep moving," he said. "We can't stop here. We have to get back to Penthos to the others."

Eden looked at Loralia and saw her eyes darken as she turned away from Azrael, stepped out of her grip, and moved quickly down the hallway. She watched as Bannack swept her into his arms for only a moment before she stepped away from him as well and continued their way down the hallway among the others. Eden followed the gentle tug of her mate's hand on her arm and they began to run down the dim hallway away from the lab where Ryan was imprisoned in the cage where he had held Aegeus for so many years. The thought made her shudder. The space had been so small, so cold, and the chains kept him brutally in place. It would have been nothing short of torture to be forced to remain in that place, unable to move more than a few inches, for years. Eden could see the pale, gruesome skin and skeletal frame that marked him as a Klimnu. Though he looked like one of the vicious creatures that had attacked her when she was first on Uoria and had caused such destruction and hardship among the entire Denynso clan for years, she knew that this man was nothing like those creatures. Yes, he was Klimnu, but Aegeus was far more. This was Maxim's father. The strong, powerful Mikana was still within him and with every breath he fought to maintain his connection to it. He refused to allow what Ryan had done to him pull him away from everything that he had ever believed and the goals that he had dedicated his life to achieve.

When she looked at Aegeus, Eden could see Maxim. The beauty was still there. The determination, gentleness, and intelligence that had made Ivy fall so deeply in love with Maxim was still evident in Aegeus's gaze and Eden felt an intense sympathy toward him. She had witnessed what happened to Maxim when he came into contact with the toxic flowers and began to change. He had fought against it with everything in him, struggling to stop the transformation and to keep himself as he was. No matter how hard he railed against the change, however, it was affecting more than just his skin. The anger, fear, and hatred that Pyra had wrongly directed at him had only fueled the transformation even further and brought the disintegration of who he was beyond his skin and into his heart. She had watched as he became angrier and more violent, and knew that if he had been left to his own devices he would have fully transformed into a Klimnu and been taken over by the vicious greed and violence that compelled those creatures. It was the love of Ivy and his determination not to justify Pyra's actions that had saved Maxim. These had kept him from disappearing completely and losing everything within him.

It was the same with Aegeus. She knew that he had clung to the love for his wife and his sons and his determination to protect his kind and everything that he had always fought for that had prevented him from giving in completely to the transformation that Ryan had tried to force on him. The corrupt scientist had tried to utilize the aggression, anger, and sadness of the Denynso to feed the change within him and send him further into the abyss of new existence as a Klimnu. The fact that Eden could still see the humanity and life in Aegeus's eyes only proved his incredible power and strength. She could see Maxim in him and could only hope that when they got him to Ciyrs, the healer would be able to restore him to his original Mikana state so that he could return to his sons and Ellora.

They reached the end of the hallway and Ciyrs and Elianna rushed toward them. Elianna swept Eden into her arms and Eden realized that she hadn't been communicating with any of them throughout the entire ordeal. She had maintained her connection with Pyra, but the stress and horror of what she was experiencing as she tried to save her son and mate from Ryan's grasp had closed off the unique connection that she had to the healer and his mate. This link had been created when she first came to be with the Denynso in the compound on Uoria. During her first encounter with the Klimnu, one of the creatures attacked her, nearly killing her. During Ciyrs's healing process he had created a close and inexplicable connection with her, somehow enabling her to communicate with him in the way that she could with Pyra. At the same time, it created the same connection with his mate, Elianna, enabling the three of them to communicate with each other freely. It was a strange ability, one that wasn't shared by any other members of the Denynso clan, and the moment marked when she changed from a human to a Denynso.

Eden stepped back from Elianna and turned to give Ciyrs a hug as well.

"Are you alright?" the healer asked, pushing her back by her upper arms and looking into her eyes. "Did he hurt you?"

Eden shook her head.

"I'm alright," she told him. "He tried, but he was more interested in Lysander and Pyra."

"Come on," Pyra said. "We need to keep going. I sincerely doubt that Ryan would only send the Valdicians to Uoria to capture Creia and not have anyone around here to guard him and his experiments. The longer we stay in place, the more vulnerable we are."

Ciyrs nodded.

"Pyra's right. We need to get back to the shuttle and get to Penthos as fast as we can." He turned toward Oro and the winged woman standing close beside him. "How did you find a shuttle to get you here so quickly?"

"We didn't take a shuttle," Oro explained.

"We took a hyper-speed vehicle," the man Ciyrs vaguely remembered as Jonah from the Nyx 23 settlement said.

"What is that?" Eden asked.

"We'll explain when we get there," Oro said.

They continued down the hallway, the group staying close together as they moved as swiftly as they could through the low light. Eden hated the shadows that filled the corners and made the doorways seem deeper. The controls were contained within an office at the front of the hallway, behind where they were traveling, so they would have to cope with the darkness until they got out of the lab and back to the university shuttle bay.

It felt strange for Eden to be running through the lab where she had once worked. Before she went to Uoria this lab had been her life. She'd spent more time in these halls and rooms than she had in her own home and felt like she could have navigated through it blindfolded. Now, though, those days of roaming the halls and dedicating all her time and energy to the research and experiments within the labs seemed like they had been lived by someone else. She could barely remember what it felt like to exist in those moments. The hallways felt strange and foreign to her and she found herself questioning each of the rooms that she passed. Though deep in the back of her mind she knew that she would be able to bring them through, it was as though she couldn't think any more than one step ahead. She couldn't see the layout of the lab in her mind or remember how to get out of it beyond taking that next step or that next turn.

Ahead of her she heard Lysander whimper and her attention focused in on him. Ty turned around and offered the infant to her. Eden gathered him into her arms and tucked him close to her chest so that she could wrap her arms around him as tightly as she could. The sound of her heartbeat and the gentle rhythm of her breaths seemed to calm him and her son fell asleep in her arms. Eden felt a surge of emotion and fought back the tears that formed in her eyes. Pyra's hand rested on her back and the weight of it comforted her and brought her focus back to getting through the corridors of the laboratory building as quickly as they could.

"What's the fastest way to get to the shuttle bay?" Gyyx asked from the front of the pack.

"Oro, you mentioned another vehicle," Pyra said. "Where is it?"

"It's right outside the shuttle bay," he said. "We were able to use tracking to get here, but the bay door was inaccessible. There's a blocking feature that prevents anyone without the proper knowledge of the machine to get to the doors. My only concern is that someone will see and destroy it."

"We'll get to it as quickly as we can," Pyra told him. "How many people can it accommodate?"

"As many as it needs to," Oro answered. "We'll figure it out when we get there."

They had reached the door at the end of the hallway that would lead them down toward the main floor of the building. Gyyx pulled on the handle, but the door didn't move.

"It's locked," he said. "It wasn't when we got here."

Eden pushed through the rest of the group to get to the

door and pressed her fingertips into the biometrics reader then input her personal code. The light on the reader should have flashed yellow then changed to green when it released the internal locking mechanism, but it didn't change from the glowing red.

"What's wrong?" Pyra asked as she tugged hard on the door with the hand that wasn't supporting Lysander.

"It won't open," she said.

George stepped up beside her and repeated the process that she had gone through. The light remained red and he glanced down at Eden questioningly before pressing his finger more insistently into the reader and imputing his personal code slowly as if to make sure that the machine was getting each of the numbers accurately.

"The lock isn't releasing," George said. "The authorized access system has been overridden."

"What does that mean?" Ty asked.

"It means that we can't open the door," Eden said.

"What?" Pyra asked, stepping forward and slamming his hand on the door. "You can't be serious."

Jonah stepped up beside Pyra and reached for the handle, shaking it briefly before pounding the keys on the number pad in random combinations.

"It wasn't locked when we got here," he said, repeating what Oro had said. "We were able to get right through."

"How did you find us?" Eden asked, a sudden sense of concern building in her mind.

"What do you mean?" Oro asked.

"How did you find us? How did you get here?"

"We told you," Jonah said. "The vehicle that we used has a built-in tracking system that allowed us to zero in on the shuttles that had traveled between the planets so that we were able to use the same path to get here."

"No," Eden said, her voice getting louder and more insistent. "Here. How did you get here? How did you find us in the laboratory? The vehicle brought you to the university, but none of you have ever been inside the laboratory buildings before. Once you were inside, how did you know where to find us?"

Oro and Jonah exchanged glances, and then looked over at Azrael and the lovely but silent winged woman who had been standing close to them since they appeared at the doorway of the lab. They all held expressions that looked as though none of them had really considered what she was asking. Oro looked back at her.

"The other doors were locked," he said.

Eden's heart started beating harder as she realized what was happening. She heard a low thud in the recesses of the building and some of the group turned toward it.

"The doors were locked?" Pyra asked.

"Yes," Oro said. "We came into the building and just started trying doors. Most of them were locked, but we found some that were open. We just kept going through the open doors."

There was another low thud, closer this time, and Eden felt prickly heat on the back of her neck.

"You didn't think that was strange?" she asked.

Jonah shook his head.

"We weren't thinking about it," he said.

"All we cared about was getting to all of you," Azrael said. "Like you said, none of us have ever been in this building. We didn't know anything about it. We thought that maybe the doors were always locked."

"They are," Eden said. There was another thud and Eden reached for Pyra's arm. "We need to go," she said. "Now."

She turned and started back down the hallway toward a short offshoot that she knew contained another access to the stairs that would lead them down to the main entrance of the building.

"What's going on, Eden?" Pyra demanded.

There was another thud, so close this time that she could nearly feel it shaking through her body.

"The doors are always locked," she said. "That's why I had to use my access code and fingerprint to get to the lab when we got there."

She tried the door to the stairwell and found it also locked.

"Then why were the others able to get through those doors?" Pyra asked.

"Ryan unlocked them," Eden said. "You said that there were only a few doors unlocked," she said, looking back at Oro. "Which ones were they?"

"The stairwells that led up," Jonah told her. "Every other floor we were able to get onto the floor and we would go down the hallway until we found another door that was open and follow that stairwell. We kept doing it until we heard your voices and then we just went toward them."

Eden handed Lysander to Pyra and pushed through the rest of the group so that she could run down the hallway toward another door.

"Why does it matter?" Gyyx asked.

"The laboratory was designed so that there are limited paths to each location within it. You can't just go from one place to another. You have to know which doors lead to which areas of the building. They created it that way to protect the labs and the research going on in them. The original building was much simpler, but scientists and their assistants were breaking into each other's labs and stealing research or sabotaging experiments. They redesigned the entire building and ensured that each person only has access to specific areas of the building."

Eden pulled on another door and it finally opened. Behind her she could hear another of the low thuds. She knew that it was the sound of the locking mechanisms within the doors somewhere in the building opening and that the only reason that that would be happening was that someone was coming through them.

2

———

Pyra followed Eden through the doorway and down the narrow stairs that led into near darkness beneath them. He could hear the fear in her voice when she was talking about the doors and the fact that she had handed him their son made him worry that there was something seriously wrong that she hadn't yet told them.

"But how were they open when Oro and the others got here, but they are locked now?" he asked.

Eden shook her head as she approached a door and pulled on it only to find that like the others it was locked.

"Ryan must have gained access to the master controls of the locks. He left the specific path of doors that would lead to his lab unlocked so that they would find us."

"But why?" George asked. "He already had Lysander and Zsilvia and me. You already knew how to get to the lab and would get there with your personal codes. He admitted that he wanted Lysander and to have us as a backup breeding couple. Wouldn't he want to prevent others from getting to us?"

"Not if he wanted to make sure that we were all vulnerable," Eden said.

"I don't understand," Pyra said. "We got out. We got him in the tank and we got away."

"We got away from the lab itself, yes," Eden said, pulling on another door until it opened. "But we haven't been able to get out of the building. Ryan said that the others are on Penthos and then Oro and the others came here and told us the same thing."

"He knew that they would come," Pyra said.

Eden stepped through the door and he followed her to the top of a stairwell leading further down into the building.

"At least he thought that they might. He knew that if there was going to be some way that they knew that we were here and in danger, however that was going to be, at least some of them would come for us. He made sure that those doors were left unlocked and that the rest weren't so that anyone who did come would be able to find us easily."

The next door that she tried opened out onto a hallway and she rushed down it. Some of the warriors followed behind while others went in the other direction, running down the opposite side of the darkened hallway pulling on the doors as they went to get them through the process more quickly. Gyyx called out to them from nearly the end of the hallway and they rushed toward him.

"Does anyone have a lightstick?" Pyra asked.

One of the warriors handed a lightstick to Pyra and he activated it. Holding it over his head to cast the light through the open doorway now in front of them, he saw that they were standing at the base of a staircase leading up.

"We just went down two flights," Gyyx said. "Why are we going up now?"

Eden shook her head and they started up the stairs.

"But we captured him," Ty pointed out. "I still don't understand the doors being unlocked and then then being locked again. And I thought that your personal code and fingerprint would unlock the doors that you were authorized to access. Why aren't they working now?"

"Ryan must have overridden the system," Eden told him. "Like I said, he planned for this. He planned for others to come. Remember that in the end what he really wants is Maxim and Kyven. The more people that he could get away from Penthos and then the more of us that he could eliminate before we had the opportunity to get back to the planet, the less of a chance there would be that we would be able to protect them from him. He might be completely deranged, but Ryan is not dumb. He knows that the Denynso are fiercely protective and that any allies that they build are going to be just as determined and driven. That is the primary reason he wanted to use them as the basis for his soldiers."

"He wants to offer up my sons to the slaughter," Aegeus said.

The sound of the Klimnu voice still made Pyra's skin crawl, but he fought to withhold the reaction. He knew that this man wasn't like the other creatures that he had encountered during the years of battle or that had nearly taken his mate from him so soon after he found her. Though his skin was grisly white and his body skeletal and misshapen, Aegeus was not the enemy that the Denynso had always perceived the Klimnu to be. In truth, he was as much a victim of the horror of the Klimnu as the Denynso. The creatures had threatened and attacked the Denynso kind, tearing their bodies and in some cases claiming their lives. At the end of the battles, though, they were able to return to their compound. They could walk away from the attacks and put them behind them, living the moments of their lives between the encounters with the creatures without the feeling of their breath on their skin or their eyes burning into theirs.

Aegeus didn't have that luxury. He was victimized in a way that Pyra couldn't even begin to imagine. The man, once a warrior so strong and powerful that even Creia respected his name, had been reduced to nothing more than a vessel. He could never escape the grotesque reality of the Klimnu. Their breath was the breath that filled his lungs and their gaze burned from his eyes. He could never walk away or put the clash with the Klimnu behind him. They had claimed his body and torn into his soul. Ryan had tried to claim his life in a way even more gruesome and horrifying than the deaths that some of the Denynso had faced. It was Aegeus, though, who had found victory over them. His body had changed, but his mind and heart had persevered.

Pyra saw Eden slow on the steps and look over her shoulder at Aegeus. Her eyes were filled with emotion as she nodded.

"Yes," she said. "If we can't make our way back to Penthos to help them and they can't get to the others on Uoria, that is exactly what is going to happen."

"But Ryan is in the tank," George said. "He's chained there."

Eden got to the top of the stairs and Pyra saw her rest her hand on the handle, hesitating for a moment as if she wasn't fully prepared to open the door and see what was waiting just beyond it. Finally, she opened it, revealing a small storage room. She rushed into it and he followed her through it back into the lab where they had faced Ryan. The warriors streamed inside and they immediately turned their attention to the tank where they had chained Ryan. It was empty.

"He's gone," Eden said, sounding desperate.

"He released the chains," Loralia said from behind Pyra, her voice weak. "I thought that they would hold him."

Pyra turned to see Bannack's arms wrapped around his mate, trying to comfort her.

"It's alright, Loralia," Eden said. "It's alright."

"He's gone!" Loralia shouted. "We don't know where he is."

The warriors suddenly erupted in shouts, and Pyra held out his hand to silence them.

"Be quiet!" he yelled. "You are doing exactly what he wants. He wants us to go against each other so that we are more vulnerable. We have to stay together and stay strong."

There was a sudden loud crash and Pyra looked up to see the door of the laboratory standing open. Four figures stepped in, each cloaked in the long black robes of the Valdicians. By their varying size and shape, however, Pyra guessed that these were not actually more of the creatures that had captured Creia on Uoria, but a few of the hybrids that Ryan had created. The lead warrior carefully handed his tiny son down to Eden and guided her back behind him without taking his eyes off the creatures that were slowly approaching them across the lab. Pyra could feel the other men around him tightening as they took hold of their weapons and prepared themselves for the conflict about to happen.

"Where do we go?" the winged woman who had come along with Oro and Jonah asked softly.

The group stepped in closer together as the Denynso warriors, Azrael, Aegeus, and Jonah moved up to the front to position the women behind them. Pyra glanced over his shoulder and saw Eden reach for one of the lab coats hanging beside her. She wrapped it tightly around her body, tying it so that it acted as a sling to hold Lysander against her and free her hands. When he turned back toward the creatures that were coming their way, he could see that each held a weapon in its hand. The hoods that they wore concealed their faces, but somehow that made them more infuriating to look at. There was no fear as he faced them down. Instead he felt only anger and the unquenchable drive to protect his family and his friends.

The clash was fierce and immediate. All at once all the men in the group surged forward and smashed into the wall created by the hybrid bodies. Pyra fought blindly. He barely knew what he was doing as his hands thrashed against them. He could feel his body coming into contact with theirs and the warmth of blood washing over his skin. The sound of screams and grunts filled the small lab around them. It was the intensity and horror of the battles that he had encountered countless times in his life condensed down into this small space and these few moments. Soon the bodies of the creatures lay battered and broken on the floor at their feet. Pyra could hear the labored breathing of the men around them and the strain in their voices told him that some were suffering injuries from the encounter.

"Pyra!"

He turned toward Eden's voice and Pyra saw worry in his mate's eyes.

"What is it?" he asked.

"You're hurt!"

Pyra glanced down and saw a narrow trickle of blood making its way down his skin, along the curve of the muscles of his forearm. He looked to Ciyrs, who was examining a deep gash in Ty's leg. The healer looked to his leader sternly.

"We need to get somewhere safe," he said. "I have to tend to these wounds."

Eden looked back at the door where they had come through from the stairwell and George started toward it.

"No," she said, reaching out to take hold of his arm. "We can't go back through there."

"Why?" Zsilvia asked.

The Denynso woman looked smaller and weaker than Pyra had ever seen her, as if the fear and strain of the day that they had just experienced had taken away all her energy. As soon as that thought went through his mind Pyra realized that he had completely lost track of time since they had been inside the laboratory building. He had no idea how long it had been since they had gotten there or how long they had fought the hybrids. It was a strange sensation and one that reminded him just how foreign Earth was to him and the rest of those who came from Uoria. When they were on their home planet they lived their lives based on the movement of the sun and the habits that they followed from day to day. Now that they were on Earth, though, he felt strangely bound by the arbitrary passage of time that they used to structure each of their daily activities. Kept away from the sun and stars inside massive, complex buildings, Pyra felt almost imprisoned by the unknown minutes and hours that passed them by.

"Ryan left those doors unlocked for a reason," she said. "He designed that path for us, knowing that eventually we would find our way back into this lab so that we could encounter those hybrids."

"But we defeated them," Pyra said.

"Those, yes," Eden said. "But I heard more than one

door open. I know that Ryan would not only send a few of his creatures to confront us. There are others and he has positioned them throughout the building to ensure that we encounter them as we are trying to get out. Remember how conniving and vicious he is. He even had a contingency plan for if the Denynso killed me when I first arrived on Uoria. He wouldn't automatically assume that he was going to be successful, or that his hybrids would be able to defeat us that easily." She shook her head and looked around at the hazy lab, the memories starting to become more obvious in her eyes. "No. He's ready. He planned for all of this. If we step back out into that stairwell, we are walking to our slaughter."

"So, what do we do?" Pyra asked. "Do we go back out the other door?"

"Yes," Eden said, nodding.

"And then what?" George asked.

She looked at him and Pyra could see an expression in her gaze that was guiding, forceful, almost as if she didn't want to say something but expected that it would occur to George if he thought about it.

"And then we go down."

3

J em checked through his bag again and then glanced around to give one final look to the cave that had been his home. He didn't know how long it had been since he had left Uoria, but in the time that he had spent on this new planet he had become accustomed to it and to the lifestyle that it had afforded him. Especially since Angela had come to be with him, even before they had completed their bond and she had become his mate, he had become comfortable and settled into his existence in the peaceful and virtually uninhabited space. Though he was excited about the possibility of returning home to Uoria and seeing his clan again, Jem still felt a pang at the thought of not ever seeing this place again.

He walked away from the cave and found Angela and Jacob standing near the creek. They both turned to watch him approach, optimistic but cautious expressions on their faces.

"Are you ready?" Angela asked.

She reached forward to take Jem's hand in hers and as soon as he felt the soft comfort of her skin against his he knew that everything was going to be fine. As long as she was standing beside him, things were going to work out exactly as they were meant to be. Even if he got back to Uoria and found that his clan had turned their back on him and that he no longer had his place there, he knew that he would still have his mate and that they could return to the planet that they had shared and make their permanent home there. He squeezed her hand and offered the best smile that he could.

"Yes," he said. "I'm ready."

"Alright," Jacob said, stepping up to them. "Then let's go."

Despite the confidence and nonchalance in the words, Jem could hear the slight hesitation in the man's voice. This would be the first time in several years that either Angela or Jacob would be on Earth. Like he had, they too had disappeared from their planet. Unlike Jem, however, their families and friends had been given false explanations as to why they had gone to the excavation deep in the desert and simply not returned. Jem struggled to decide which would be more difficult, them returning to lives that had been manipulated and damaged by those who didn't want anyone to know that they had truly disappeared from the research site, or him returning to the life that his kind thought had ended the moment that he fell from the limb in the mirrored realm beneath the Denynso compound. Their family and friends thought that they had moved on into a new life and had simply been living without them. To them, Angela and Jacob had purposely left them and would be returning to the life that they abandoned. To the Denynso clan, however, Jem would be stepping out of death and back into a life that had likely already been put to rest.

Jem looked at each of them and Jacob and Angela

stepped up closer to him so that they were a tight cluster, their shoulders touching as they all focused on the necklace that Jem wore around his neck. He lifted the small metal cage and looked in at the piece of wall that it contained. This had once been a reminder of the first cave that he had settled into when he arrived on this planet and resigned himself to the reality that he would never be able to return to Uoria. Now he understood it as the method by which he would get back to the planet that he loved and the people he had thought of each day since inadvertently leaving them behind.

"Are you ready?" he asked them, repeating the question that they had asked him to ensure that all three were prepared for the brief but largely unknown journey that lay ahead of them.

Angela and Jacob both nodded and Jem returned the gesture before opening the metal cage so that they could access the piece of wall within. Ensuring that their bodies were touching, the three reached forward and touched their fingertips to the engravings in the stone that marked this small segment of stone the portal that would bring them directly back to Earth.

Jem closed his eyes as the tugging feeling began in his chest and traveled through his body until he felt as though everything inside of him was moving away from his body. A few moments later, he felt his body catch up with the pull from within him and the dizzy, near-blackness in his mind that told him that they would soon arrive in the museum. He struggled to maintain his connection with what was around him. In the times that he had used the portals to move from this planet to Earth and then to Vyker's stream and back he had learned that the transition could be extremely difficult on their bodies. He had seen the detrimental effects on Galadriel and worried that the same thing could happen to him if he wasn't vigilant about his mind and body and how they responded to the transition. Jem kept his mind moving as quickly as he could, forcing thoughts through it nearly indiscriminately in the few moments that it took for them to move through the portal.

Finally, he felt his body hit something solid and knew that they had made it to Earth. Jem lay still for a few seconds, giving himself a chance to recover from the transition and acclimate to being on the planet. When he felt his body relax, he opened his eyes and looked to the side to make sure that Angela and Jacob had both fared the journey well. Jacob was propped up on his elbow rubbing his forehead, but Angela was still lying on her back, her eyes closed. A sense of panic rushed through him as Jem remembered how Galadriel looked when they had traveled from the museum to Vyker's stream. She had looked very much like Angela did now, eyes closed and skin pale, only to be revived quite some time later after being brought to Vyker's home.

Jem knelt at Angela's side and rested his hand to the side of her face, then ran it across her forehead. Her eyes fluttered open and he felt relief flood through his body. Jem leaned down to rest a kiss to her lips as she smiled up at him.

"Let's keep moving," Jacob said in a hushed voice. "We probably don't want the guards to find us wandering through the museum when it's closed."

With that, Jem looked around and realized that the corridor where they had arrived was shadowy with only small lights along the ceiling glowing in the darkness. It had been like this when he came with Vyker and Galadriel, but he couldn't remember where they went or what they had done when they were there. It was an uncomfortable realization. As a Denynso warrior he had been trained to be aware of his surroundings and respond. Now that he was back in the museum he knew that he hadn't used this training when he was first in the museum, putting him in the unpleasant situation of not knowing where he was or what might happen as they made their way through the darkened building.

"Where should we go from here?" he asked.

"I think that it would be best to get out of the museum," Jacob said. "We can decide what to do from there. If the guards caught us in here, we would have a lot more trouble on our hands, especially considering that Angela and I are supposed to be in other parts of the world and you are from another planet and suspected dead. We get out first, then we figure out how to get to Uoria."

4

George could see the storm of emotion in Eden's eyes. He knew that she wasn't completely confident in what she was saying. The thought of stepping outside of the lab was frightening. He knew that the creatures that Ryan had talked about, more of what they had already encountered, were waiting for them throughout the building, and it likely didn't matter which direction that they went. The chances that they were going to be able to get out without finding more of them were slim. Eden, however, knew the way that Ryan thought better than anyone. If she believed that it would be more dangerous for them to leave through the staircase that they had used to get into the lab, they needed to listen to her.

"Down?" he asked. "Toward the main doors?"

Eden shook her head.

"Not yet," she answered. "They will be staking out every single entrance and exit to this building that they know about. If we go to the main doors, we'll have to go through the lobby, which means there will be nothing to protect us."

"That they know about?" Pyra asked.

Eden let out a breath and nodded. The blend of emotion in her eyes had seemed to fracture slightly, spreading out into more identifiable thoughts and feelings for a brief moment, and in them George could see fear simmering within them. It was a different type of fear than some might have expected to see in the eyes of a young mother facing such intense danger. It was guarded, as if the determination to defeat what had tormented her when she was on Earth and protect the home and family that she had built when she finally left the life behind had created a barrier around the fear and wasn't allowing it to control her.

"There are sections of the building that most people don't know about," she said. "Even I haven't been into them."

"Then how do you know that they are there?" George asked.

She looked at him with that same expression that told him that he should know what she was talking about.

"I don't know for sure," Eden said carefully, "but for now, it's really the only option that we have."

Without waiting for anyone to say anything to her, she crossed the room and rested her hand on the doorknob. She paused for only a moment, leaning toward the door as if listening for any movement that might be on the other side, and then opened the door. George could feel all the men around him brace themselves, preparing for the swarm of hybrids to come into the room, but none did. They left the room again and rushed out into the hallway. It felt strange to be following the same path that they already had, but there was no choice. Ryan had them like rats in a maze. At this moment, they were completely at the mercy of the building and of his whim; the only choice that they had was to follow the thoughts of Eden, who seemed even more driven now.

They followed the corridor until they reached an exit at the end in the opposite direction that they had originally gone. George noticed that there was no keypad beside it and realized that it might be a storage closet. There were doors similar to that on the floor of the building where he had his lab and offices, but they had long since been emptied and abandoned, or filled with crates of decades-old records being used in research projects. He knew that most of these closets throughout the building were rarely used and even when they were they didn't contain anything that was sensitive or confidential, which is why they didn't bother with keypads and personal access codes. This closet, though, seemed intriguing to Eden. She was staring at it in a way that told him she knew something about it that the others didn't.

"What is it, Eden?" Pyra asked, stepping up beside Eden as she rested her hand to the door.

"What if he knows?" she murmured to herself.

It was hard to tell if she was speaking to herself or the others, but Pyra brought his strong hand to her back and guided her up against himself comfortingly.

"What if he knows what?" he asked. "Ryan? Are you talking about Ryan?"

Eden nodded and looked over her shoulder at him. She seemed to be opening her mouth as if to saying something but then there was an extremely loud crashing sound in the direction of the stairwell and her eyes widened. Without another word of explanation, she pulled open the door and revealed that it was, in fact, a closet. There were a few crates sitting on the floor and pieces of outdated equipment shrouded in cloths tucked in the corner. Eden began to pull on one of the large pieces and Pyra guided her aside by her shoulders so that she was out of the closet. George saw her wrap her arms protectively around Lysander where he was tied to her chest and lean down to touch a kiss to the top of his head. It was difficult to see, a moment so tender and gentle, and yet so heavy with the emotion and energy of what was happening around them.

George stepped into the closet with Pyra and helped him move the objects inside out, handing them over to the other men in the group. Gyyx tossed one of the boxes behind them and the sound of its impact on the floor shuddered through the building.

"No, Gyyx!" Eden hissed. "We can't call attention to ourselves."

"I'm sorry," the massive warrior said.

He took another box from Ty and lowered it more carefully to the ground. They listened for a moment and heard another crash in the distance, sounding even closer this time than the one before. It seemed Eden had been right and the hybrids had been lurking in the staircase, waiting for them to come back in so that they could ambush them. Now that they hadn't, the creatures were making their way back up to the laboratory. The thought suddenly shot through George's mind that they still didn't know where Ryan had gone. He could be truly anywhere at this point. If he had actually figured out how to override the locking system of the building he had access to anywhere he wanted to go, which meant that he could move through the building at his whim, coming at them from any direction he pleased.

They moved more quickly getting the rest of the boxes and equipment out of the closet and stepped out of the way so that Eden could go inside again. She walked to the far end and ran her hand along the wall carefully as if feeling for something in the paint. Finally, she stopped and applied pressure to the wall. Nothing happened and she moved her hands to the side and pressed again.

"What are you doing?" George asked.

"Give me a minute," Eden snapped and moved her hands slightly again.

She pressed again and there was a slight cracking sound. Seeming motivated by the reaction, Eden lifted her hands and slammed them against the wall. Long, meandering cracks appeared in the paint and Eden repeated the gesture. Pyra stepped into the closet with her and reached up to dig his fingers into the cracks being formed by Eden's hands. His thick fingers pulled away at the paint and the wall material beneath it. As it fell away George realized that the pieces were nowhere near as thick as they should be. Pyra continued pulling at the wall and within a few moments they had revealed a large hole.

"Holy shit," he muttered. "What is that?"

There was a slight smile on Eden's face. It wasn't one of happiness, but rather relief, as if she had not fully believed what she had been thinking when she first stepped into the closet. She reached for the lightstick that Pyra had tucked into the waistband of his pants and climbed through the hole. The darkness engulfed her, but a moment later she held the light up above her head rather than in front of her and the glow illuminated an old, narrow staircase. A gasp rippled through the group and George felt a glimmer of excitement and hope in his belly.

"Let me go first," Pyra demanded, and Eden stepped out of his way.

The warrior started down the stairs, ducking down and turning slightly sideways to accommodate his tremendous size as he made his way along them. Eden fell into step behind him and George followed, reaching behind him for Zsilvia's hand. He knew that she would be there without even having to look. The connection that they had between them was far more powerful than anything that he had ever experienced. It was unexplainable how closely tied he felt to her and the way that they seemed to exist in the same moments, the same breaths. They seemed to orbit each other, always knowing where the other was and being able to move together without having to find each other. His hand wrapped around hers and he felt her body come up close behind him.

"Where does that lead?" she whispered.

George shook his head.

"I don't know," he admitted. "I've never seen it before. I don't know why it's there."

They stepped into the stairwell and followed the sound of Pyra's footsteps in the darkness ahead of them. He used the hand that wasn't holding Zsilvia's to guide himself along the handrail to one side. The metal pole felt cold, gritty, and sticky with cobwebs. It was evident that it had been many years since any other hand had used this rail as someone walked down the stairs. That was at once unnerving and comforting. Though it meant that they were moving into a section of the building that had been abandoned, meaning it might be unstable and filled with unknown dangers, it also meant that no one else had found that stairwell. This was reassuring, telling him that neither Ryan nor his hybrid creatures had used these stairs and they may be moving into an area that would keep them safe as they tried to escape the laboratory and get back to the ships to bring them to Penthos.

The group made their way down the stairs as quickly as they could. George followed them nearly blindly. Eden had moved far enough ahead of him that he couldn't see the light from the lightstick and he only had the sound of the footsteps and heavy breaths ahead of him to keep him going. He didn't know how far they would need to go. He simply let his feet follow them and waited for them to end. The stairs turned at points, following sharp bends that seemed to indicate that they were moving through the different floors of the building. There were not enough of them, however, to mimic the floors of the laboratory that they had already followed, indicating that wherever in the building they were, it was different form the section to which they were already accustomed.

Finally, ahead of him he heard the footsteps stop.

"There's another door, Pyra," Eden said. "Is it unlocked?"

"No," Pyra said. "It doesn't matter."

There was a tremendous crashing sound and George knew that the Denynso warrior had kicked down the door. If it was anything similar to the lightweight closet door that they had encountered before entering the hidden stairwell, this would not have been a challenge. Almost instantly George's lungs filled with thick, dusty air and he muffled a cough against his arm. The air smelled old, like it had been closed behind that door for quite some time without benefit of moving in and out of lungs or moving with an open window.

"We need more light," Eden called from ahead of him.

George relayed the message to the group behind him and soon there were several other pinpoints of light shining over his shoulder.

"Not all of them," Pyra said. "Those have traveled a far way without charging and we need to conserve the light."

A few of the lights turned off and George felt a tap on his shoulder. He turned and took the light that Ty was handing him so that he could pass it along to Pyra. A moment later they started moving again. Soon George stepped down off the final stair and felt himself surrounded by the stale air. The glow from another lightstick behind him revealed the outline of the broken door and he could see a large expanse of darkness beyond it. The shifting light that broke through the darkness told him that Pyra and Eden were standing slightly apart in the space and moving their lightsticks around to scan the room.

George gently pulled on Zsilvia's hand as he guided her further into the space and away from the door so that the others could join them. As soon as he was inside, he realized that the room that they were in was not as large as he thought that it was. Once the rest of the group was inside, he could feel their bodies close to him and could only walk a few steps to either side before encountering them.

"What now?" a voice came from the other side of the room.

"There has to be another door," Eden replied. "We find it and we keep going."

"What do we do about the door?" George asked. "Just leave it?"

"We can't," Gyyx said. "They'll find it. We need to cover our tracks as much as possible."

In the faint light from the lightstick beside him, George saw Azrael step back out of the broken door and heard his footsteps rushing up the stairs. Around him the others had gone to action exploring the room and soon he heard Ty and Ciyrs call to Pyra.

"There are some old shelves over here," Ciyrs called. "We can move them in front of the door. It might not stop them for long, but it will block it long enough to slow them down."

"We have to wait for Azrael," Oro said.

Only moments later George could hear the footsteps again and the winged man ducked back into the room.

"I closed the door to the closet and blocked it with some of the equipment so even if they do open it, they will have to move them out of the way to find the gap in the wall."

Eden nodded.

"Thank you, Azrael," she said. "We need to get these shelves in front of the door. Zsilvia, Elianna, help me find a door out of here."

Zsilvia's hand left George's as she moved toward Eden. He started toward the warriors and grabbed onto one of the tall sets of metal shelves that had been discarded in the corner of the room. Together they carried the shelves over to the door and positioned them so that four lay on their sides across the door with two more standing vertically in front of them. Gyyx lifted another set and slid it over the tops of the other shelves, following it with another so that those two wedged tightly into place between the other shelves and the ceiling. It would take strength and time to get past the barrier. This at once gave George a sense of security and reminded him that they were moving deeper into a space that was completely unfamiliar.

"Here's the door," Elianna called and the group rushed toward her.

George could see an extremely outdated version of the keypad beside the door, but it was clear that it was no longer connected. Eden took hold of the handle and the door immediately opened. They pushed through into another corridor and something seemed familiar to George. He pushed back out of the corridor into the room. He felt for the bag that he had grown accustomed to wearing at his hip since being on Uoria and realized that it wasn't there. He remembered that he hadn't carried it with him when he and Zsilvia came back to the lab before the wedding, and the lack of it made him feel angrier. Without the tools that he usually carried, he felt vulnerable and ineffective. Though he had never carried such items when he was at this laboratory before he went to Uoria, after his time on the planet he had developed a deep need to always feel prepared. Being there and engaging with the other species had brought a greater understanding of himself and awareness of his being in connection with others and with the world around him. Before he left Earth, his life had been controlled only by his mind and the research that defined him. After arriving on Uoria and meeting the Denynso, bonding with Zsilvia, and seeing the conflicts and clashes that had unfolded, however, he seemed to awaken to the presence and power of his body. No longer did he immediately go only to the logic and knowledge that he held as the only way that he would be able to help in any situation. Instead, conflict and challenges triggered a compulsion to protect, to work, and to fight. His mind and body had connected and he relied on the tools that he carried with him to allow him to react to whatever they encountered.

Now that he was without his bag and everything that he had carried inside it, he felt thrown back into the life that he had had before he left Earth. He hated the feeling of emptiness and this fueled his hatred toward Ryan even further.

"Can I use your lightstick?" he asked Ty.

The warrior handed him the light and George rushed back into the room. He held the light up over his head and turned so that it scanned across the walls around him. As he oriented himself to face the door where the rest of the group was streaming into the corridor, the light fell onto a boarded-up window. Another was several inches away; the crumbling remains of a counter sticking jaggedly out from beneath it. This was a medical wing.

5

Eden moved along the corridor cautiously. The space was heavy with the feeling of abandonment, carrying that strange sense of memory that always seemed to linger in places like this. It was as if there had been such a concentration of life and energy there that it had saturated the walls, the floor, and the air itself, allowing the space to hold on to every moment that it had experienced so that even long after those moments ended, it didn't forget.

The floor beneath her feet was made of scuffed cream-colored polished cement and in the light of the stick in her hand she could see that the walls to either side were made of ceramic tiles. The tiles were crumbling in some places, further underscoring how long it had been since anyone had walked along this hall. There were closed doors every few feet on either side of her, some featuring small plaques with combinations of letters and numbers that she could only imagine were once a classification system to manage the rooms. Part of her wanted to try to open the doors, but another hesitated, unsure of what she would find if the doors were unlocked as the one leading from the small room had been. Finally, she knew that she couldn't keep hesitating. They didn't know where they were or what these rooms were, and they would need to find out if they were going to have any chance of making their way out of the building before Ryan or the hybrids caught up with them.

A set of large double doors loomed ahead of her. She wouldn't allow herself to hesitate. Pressing Lysander tightly to her with one hand, she pushed through the doors with the other, immediately thrusting the lightstick into the darkness ahead. The door opened out into an even wider hallway lined with more doors. Above her she could see old lights embedded in the ceiling and remnants of what looked like some kind of intercom or communication system positioned in the empty spaces between the rooms. It was an eerie feeling that made the tips of her fingers tingle and her mind intensely aware of each of her senses as if preparing her to respond to whatever the next step would trigger.

"Eden," George's voice called from behind her.

She turned and saw the man pushing through the rest of the group to her.

"Are you alright?" she asked as he approached.

"This is a medical ward," he told her.

"What?" she asked.

"A medical ward," George repeated. "That room that we found is an old registration room. I saw the windows in the wall."

"This laboratory building doesn't have a medical ward," Eden protested.

"Not anymore," Jonah said.

Eden turned to Jonah. The young man was walking toward her, an indecipherable expression on his face.

"What do you mean?" she asked.

"Before my crew left for our mission, we had our head-quarters in the same complex as the old university. The buildings were actually connected by skywalks. One of the university buildings was a hospital."

"But the old university was demolished," George said. "It was torn down decades ago so that they could build the new university. All of the buildings in the complex came down."

"No," Jonah said, shaking his head. "They might have taken down some of the buildings, but for some reason they kept the hospital. This is the old medical ward. I remember coming into it a few times. When we first got here, I thought that it was the same area as the headquarters building and university, but none of the buildings looked familiar. Now that I'm here, though, I know exactly where I am. This laboratory is far bigger than the hospital was, but this," he gestured around him, "this is the hospital that was here when I was. It was old even then. They had tried to do some improvements. These keypads look similar to the technology that was implemented just when we left. A lot of the building was already totally outdated, though."

"So why did they keep it?" Pyra asked. "If it was already so old, why wouldn't they take it down when they took down the other buildings?"

Jonah looked around.

"I don't know. It doesn't make any sense. Why would they seal up an abandoned hospital and build a new laboratory off of it?"

"What's in these rooms?" Ciyrs asked, gesturing toward one of the doors.

The healer sounded intrigued by the idea of an Earth medical facility. On Uoria, Ciyrs performed his healing treatments in a small clinic attached to his home if they were in the compound. Otherwise, he used his inborn powers or the ointments and medicines that he crafted wherever he needed to, to heal and protect the warriors or whoever needed it. This was the first time that he had the opportunity to see where Earth doctors and surgeons used their skills, as outdated as it may be.

"These are examination rooms," Eden explained. "It's where the doctors would see their patients."

Ciyrs stepped up to one of the rooms and tried the handle. The door opened and Eden came to his side to hold her light up for him to see. The room beyond the door was filled with old chairs. They looked like they had been tossed into the room haphazardly, filling the space with leaning, precarious towers.

"Those were in the waiting room," Jonah said. "I remember what they looked like sitting out there."

His voice had become softer as if he were talking to her through the years that had passed since the last time he had stood in that building. They kept walking down the hallway, opening the doors to the examination rooms as they went. Some were completely empty while others held remnants of what the medical facility used to be, including stacked beds, file cabinets, and tangles of equipment. They paused in front of one of the doors and Jonah ran his fingers along the plaque. He gave a soft, mirthless laugh.

"This is the room where I got my final clearance exam before boarding for the Nyx 23 mission," he said. "Since it was a clandestine mission, we couldn't all go in together for our examinations like we usually did before a voyage. For the few weeks leading up to the launch a couple of us a day would come in and get examined, pretending it was just a regular department checkup. I was the last one."

He reached for the handle of the door and pushed, but it didn't move. He tried again and Eden could hear the clicking of the mechanisms inside the door that told her that the door was locked. She stepped aside and Pyra planted his boot just below the handle, forcing the lock out of place.

The door opened, revealing an intact examination room. Eden was startled by the appearance of the space. Of every room along the corridor, this was the only one that still looked like it would have when the hospital was still in operation. Jonah's eyes narrowed as he hesitantly stepped over the threshold into the room as if he was being drawn back into the last time he had gone into the room. Eden tried to reconcile the reality that when Jonah had attended that appointment before leaving for the mission, it was years before even her grandparents were born. When he stepped into that room, ready for the same type of examination he had undergone many times before in preparation for missions. He knew that there was a voyage ahead and that it would be unlike anything that he had experienced before as they ventured to an unknown planet. She wondered if he had been nervous, if there had been even the slightest indication that this mission wouldn't go the way that the others had, that he wouldn't return until more than a century later.

Jonah crossed to the bed positioned in the center of the room and rested his hand on the mattress. The sheets and blanket had been pulled tightly and tucked in severe corners, the pillow rested at the head of the bed as if awaiting the next patient. Whoever had prepared the room for the hospital to close hadn't treated it like the room would never been used again. Instead, it had been put back together just as it would have been at the end of any other day, ready for the next morning.

"This is so strange," Jonah said. "Why this room? Of all the rooms on this floor, why did they keep this room like this?" He looked at the counter on one wall and Eden followed his gaze to the canisters and boxes of medical implements arranged neatly on the surface. A slim silver case sat in the center of the counter and even from the distance Eden could see the coating of dust over it. "Look at this," Jonah said, walking up to the counter. "They even left a patient file just sitting out on the counter."

"Wouldn't they bring something like that with them when they moved to the new facility?" Eden asked.

"I would think so," Jonah answered.

He picked the metal file up and brushed away the dust on the front. Eden saw his hand pause and his head lean slightly closer to the front of the file. He continued to brush away the dust with greater intensity and then Eden saw his hand begin to shake.

"Jonah?" she said. "Jonah, what is it?"

She stepped up to his side and held the lightstick up higher. The glow fell on the file in his hand. It was an old-fashioned version of a patient file, a design that hadn't been used in many years but might have still been in use when the old hospital had been closed many years before. She looked more closely at it and immediately saw what had caused Jonah to pause. There was a name engraved on the front of the file as it would have been on every permanent patient filed. *Jonah Kenyon.*

Eden remembered the first time that she had seen Jonah in the settlement on Uoria. Though she hadn't realized what it was at the time because they didn't yet know that these were not only humans but the members of a lost mission from a century before, he had been wearing a shirt that featured a remnant of his uniform stitched together with other pieces of fabric. On that scrap had been two letters. JK.

"What is it?" George asked from behind them.

Eden took the file from Jonah's hand and turned to show it to George.

"It's his patient folder," Eden said.

"What?" George asked.

"It's my patient folder," Jonah reiterated. "The doctor put it right there on the counter at the end of my examination before we left for Penthos."

"That can't be," Eden said, shaking her head. "The hospital was open for years after the Nyx 23 mission. At least a decade, maybe a little more."

"I remember when he put it there," Jonah said. "He input the information from my tests, scanned my fingerprints, and sent all of the information to the command leader, then closed the file and put it down right here."

"The command leader?" Eden asked. "The department head?"

Jonah shook his head.

"No. Nyx 23 was a clandestine mission even within the department itself. The department head and the governing bodies didn't want anything to do with Penthos or with the Valdicians. Nyx 23 was a small faction within the larger group and planned the mission."

Jonah opened the file and pressed the button that would have once started the file, but it remained dark.

"It's been more than 100 years," Eden said. "The energy cells would have worn out."

As if the words triggered him, Lysander began to cry. She patted him gently, but his wails only grew louder. The more he cried, the more aware she became of the exhaustion that was coursing through her own body. The voices around her started to sound muffled and the light faded as her eyes started to close.

"We need to get somewhere to rest," Pyra said.

"No," Eden said, her voice weak even as she tried to sound as insistent as she could. "We have to keep going. We have to get to the others."

"Eden," Pyra said over Lysander's cries. "Listen to your son. He needs to be changed and fed. He needs to sleep somewhere where he isn't being jostled around."

"We have to get out of here," she said. "Jonah has been here before, he can get us out."

"I've only been to this floor," Jonah said. "I know that the other floors have other rooms, but we don't know how much of the original structure was kept or what type of condition it's in. I wouldn't know how to navigate us out of here completely on my own."

"What do you think are the chances that anyone else knows about this?" Pyra asked, turning his attention to George.

Eden could see George glance around as if he himself was still shocked by the fact that they were inside the long-abandoned medical building.

"I don't know," George said. "I definitely didn't know about it and I've been working in this lab far longer than Ryan."

"Eden, how did you know about it?" Pyra asked.

Eden was starting to feel dizzy. It was as if the nearly two days that had passed since she had slept had all just pounded down into her and were making it so that she could barely stand. She shook her head slightly.

"I don't know," she said. "I don't remember. I heard about it somewhere. It was just a rumor, but I remember thinking that it seemed strange."

"What seemed strange?"

"The closets," she said. "Why so many closets?"

Lysander's cries seemed to pull away from her, disappearing into the distance as her consciousness pulled her away from the others like she was being pulled backward through a tunnel. She felt her body weaken and her legs give out. All she could do was scoop one arm around the baby as she collapsed toward the ground.

6

———

Jem pressed himself to the wall, trying to make himself as small as possible so that he could disappear into the shadows. He could hear the footsteps of the guard making his rounds through the gallery and he held his breath as they got closer. Behind him Angela and Jacob crouched in the recesses of an exhibit, their smaller forms making it far easier for them to be unassuming in the stillness of the closed museum. Finally, the guard passed by them and the sound of his shoes grew fainter in the distance as he made his way deeper into the galleries that wrapped around the center of the hall. Jem gestured for the others to follow and they rushed into the vulnerability of the open halls. Though he didn't think that there was more than that one guard patrolling this wing of the museum, Jem couldn't be sure, which meant that they had to stay cautious until they were safely out of the building.

"Which way do we go now?" he asked in as soft a whisper as he could manage while still making sure that the others heard him.

"There's a sign," Angela said, pointing several feet ahead of him and up on a wall.

Staying crouched low to the floor, Jem scurried toward the sign and looked up at it. Jacob came up beside him and pointed at the top word.

"Lobby," he said.

That wasn't a word used on Uoria, but Jem took Jacob's gesture and the way that Angela began to move in the direction of the arrow on the sign to mean that that was where they would find the exit. They moved as swiftly as they could and relief washed over him when he saw a wide, open area with a bank of doors ahead of them. He remembered this space. He and Galadriel had run across it during his first visit to the museum and escaped through those doors that stood just on the other side.

"Wait," Jacob said when Jem made a move to cross the atrium. "There's a guard at the front desk."

That guard hadn't been stationed there before and Jem could only imagine that his position had been added after Galadriel and he had simply unlocked the doors and run out amid the screaming of the alarm. Jem looked at the doors, narrowing his eyes to see them in as much detail as he could at the distance, and noticed that they were much the same as they had been the last time. Tall and wide, the doors were made up mostly of glass with the exception of black sections of metal across the center. It was on those metal sections where Galadriel had released the lock. Jem looked back at the guard. He knew that they weren't going to have the luxury of enough time to pause and unlock the door before getting out.

The desk with the guard was positioned at the far side of the lobby, tucked to the side of the bank of doors so that he would have full view of anyone going into or out of the building. This meant that he was several yards away from the far doors, which meant that he would have to move around the large, nearly full-circle desk and then across the room in order to get to them if they were to go for the doors at the furthest end.

"How do we get there?" he asked, pointing in the direction of another corridor that fed out into the lobby closer to the far doors.

Angela looked down the hall where they were crouched and then back toward the sign.

"It looks like the galleries wrap around," she said. "If we keep following this hall, eventually it will lead us through the exhibits and to that hallway. There will be other guards in those wings, though," she said. "Museums spread them out so that they can keep the entire building under surveillance."

Jem nodded.

"We're just going to have to be careful," he said. "We don't really have much of an option."

Angela and Jacob nodded at him and they started their way down the hallway again. Jem's heart pounded in his chest as they crept through the corridors and galleries. It was as though he could feel the pendant around his neck jump with each beat, reminding him heavily of the journey that he had already taken and the one that still lay before him. As they moved through the museum he found his mind reaching out to the displays that they passed as if trying to capture any little pieces of information that it could about the different times and places that they memorialized. Everything seemed so much larger now, so much more complex than he had ever considered before he left Uoria. Just as they made their way into the final corridor, he wondered if somewhere deep in the museum, in a section that they hadn't yet explored, there was an exhibit about the Denynso, and if there was, what it would say and how it would present his warrior kind.

When they finally reached the end of the hall, Jem, Angela, and Jacob huddled together behind a section of the wall that jutted out into the entrance to make a large, imposing arch. Angela looked around his arm at the doors and then up at Jem's face.

"What now?" she asked. "The guard is right there."

Jem looked at the guard and then back at the doors. They seemed further away from the corridor than they had when he first saw them, but this was their only chance. They had no other option for how to get out of the museum and every moment that they spent inside made it more likely that one of the other guards would discover them. The locking mechanism on the doors was more complex than it had been and it was even clearer now that they wouldn't have time to even attempt to unlock them. He took a breath and stood.

"Now," he said, "we run."

Jem shot out of the shadows without another moment of hesitation, hoping that the others would follow him. He squared his body toward the door, brought his arms up cover his face, and leapt. There was a brief moment of stillness before he encountered the glass. In the next instant, he felt the pane splintering around him and heard the familiar screaming of the alarm accented by the glass falling to the ground. He hit the ground, but got up instantly to turn and make sure that Angela and Jacob were making their way out.

Through the other doors Jem could see the guard running from his desk toward the door, a communicator held to his mouth. The door had broken in such a way that the metal bar across the middle was bent but still intact, but most of the glass was gone from both the top and bottom sections Jacob was climbing over the metal as Angela scrambled across the ground to get out through the bottom. They both got to their feet and came running toward him seconds before the guard reached the door. Jem latched on to Angela's wrist and he scooped her up into his arms as he took off running down the steps in front of the museum and down the sidewalk.

They ran until they reached a corner, then turned, starting a weaving path through the neighborhood surrounding the museum until he could hear Jacob's footfalls slow and then stop. Jem stopped and walked back to Jacob before lowering Angela to the ground.

"They won't find us," Jacob reassured them. "They'll look around the museum and in the immediate area, but until they watch the cameras, they don't even know who they're looking for."

"When they do, it will pretty hard to miss Jem," Angela said.

Jem felt a tinge of guilt, but then saw his mate smile. He reached down for her hands and turned them over to look at her palms.

"Are you alright?" he asked. "Did you cut yourself?"

"Only a little," Angela said. "I'll be alright."

"Let's get somewhere where I can bandage those for you," Jem said.

They started walking down the sidewalk and a few moments later noticed what looked like a small restaurant. A sign glowed in the window and the faint sound of music came toward them as they approached.

"Are they open?" Jacob asked.

"It looks like it," Angela replied.

Jem pulled the door open and the three stepped inside. He immediately noticed that they were the only people there with the exception of a grizzled man standing behind a long, narrow table that curved around the far end of the room. He lifted his eyes to the three of them as they walked in and his gaze focused directly on Jem. The warrior could feel the man evaluating him, scrutinizing him in much the same way that Angela and Jacob had when they first saw him. He anticipated a strong, possibly even violent, reaction, but there was none. The man simply gestured at the tables scattered around the room and then went back to cleaning the glass he held in one hand.

The three of them went to one of the tables and sat down, dropping their bags at their feet. Jem reached into his and drew out some of the bandages he had packed. He spread them across the table and then took out a cloth. Without warning the man appeared at the side of the table and place a large glass of water in front of Jem. He nodded toward Angela's hands.

"Everything alright?" he asked in a voice that was exactly what Jem anticipated would have come out of him.

"Yes," Jem replied. "She cut herself on some glass. I'm just going to bandage her up."

"Can I help you with anything?" the man asked.

His tone was long and slow, the words grumbling in his throat long after he said them, but there was something about them that sounded sincere and Jem shook his head.

"No," he said. "Thank you."

The man gave a single nod and walked away from the table. The interaction gave Jem a sense of comfort that he couldn't really explain, and he felt more secure and calm as he went to work rinsing Angela's hands with the water that the man had brought them.

"What do we do from here?" Jacob asked.

Jem started winding one of the bandages around Angela's hand and shook his head.

"I don't know," he admitted. "Now that we're here, I don't know any more how to get back to Uoria than I did when we were on our planet."

"I think the best way is going to be through the University," Angela said. "They have connections with Uoria and with your king. They might even have another group preparing to travel there for the exchange program, and if they don't they might be able to charter a special flight specifically for you considering the circumstances."

"Do you know how to get there from here?" Jem asked.

"We can't walk," Angela admitted. "We need a car."

"Maybe we should get in touch with Rilex," Jacob suggested. "Galadriel asked him to take care of her car and her apartment and everything when she and Ty decided to stay with Vyker. Maybe he would help us."

Jem wasn't sure how he felt about reaching out to Rilex. Convincing her that his name was Rick and that he was a researcher who shared her fascination with the wall that had eventually brought her to Vyker and then to Jem, Rilex eventually admitted that he was actually one of Vyker's species, the best friend of his father who had disappeared many years before. Though he had been extremely helpful to them in their efforts to restore the Star Wall and protect the universe from the StarKillers, Rilex had also been somewhat cool toward Jem, almost as though he were suspicious of the Denynso. He had chosen to return to Earth even after Ty and Galadriel agreed to stay with Vyker, which had struck Jem as strange, though now with the sense of attachment that he felt for the jungle planet where he had spent so much time since his own disappearance, he thought he might at least somewhat understand.

"How do we do that?" Angela asked.

Jacob reached into his bag and pulled out what looked like a small journal.

"This," he said with a hint of a smile on his lips. "Galadriel gave it to me before I left to visit you."

"What is it?" Jem asked.

Angela took the journal from Jacob's hands and opened it.

"This is Galadriel's journal," she said. "It has Rilex's contact information in it. Why would she give this to you?"

"She said that I should have it with me just in case I needed it. That I could give it back to her when she saw me again. It was almost like she knew that we were going to come here."

"How could she have known?" Jem asked. "Even I didn't know."

Angela's eyes dropped to the necklace that he still wore around his neck and then lifted back to his.

"Home is always home," she said.

The man from behind the bar appeared at the side of the table again and rested his hand to the table. When he moved it away there was a small black metal piece sitting on the surface. He made eye contact with Jem and then walked away again. Jem felt like the man had been listening to them, but even though it should have bothered him, he was also strangely grateful for his presence.

"What is that?" Jem asked as Angela reached for the object that the man had left behind.

"It's a phone," she said. "We can call Rilex."

Jem didn't fully understand what she meant, but then she picked up the device and input the combination of numbers that were on the page in the journal. A moment later he heard a buzzing sound coming from the phone and then a slight click followed by a familiar voice.

"Hello?" Rilex said with a slight tinge of confusion in his words. "This is Rick Abernathy."

He was using the human name he had chosen for himself when he arrived on Earth many years before after accidentally traveling through a portal, much as Jem had when he left Uoria during the battle with the Klimnu. That was the name that Jem had first used to refer to him, but it had never really fit him. Even though he looked fully human, there was something about him that had always struck him as different, as if because he, too, was a different species he was able to detect others. Soon, though, he found out that the man's name was actually Rilex and that had been lying about his identity to manipulate Galadriel's movements in an effort to complete the task that he had set out to do in a different time, in a different version of reality. Though the idea was difficult to wrap his head around when he first heard it, somehow it made everything fall into place. Suddenly his disappearance from Uoria and his arrival on the unknown jungle planet had begun to make sense.

"Rilex, this is Angela."

There was a brief pause before Rilex replied.

"Angela!" he said with excitement. "Where are you?"

"We're in a bar somewhere in the neighborhood with the museum. It's the only place we could find that's open."

"Perfect, stay where you are."

"What?" Angela said, but there was another slight click and she looked down at the phone with an expression that told Jem that the call had ended. "He hung up."

"Why does he want us to stay here?" Jacob asked.

Angela shook her head. Jem reached across the table to

hold her hand, finding comfort in the feeling of her skin. It was still so strange to think that she had only been his mate for such a short time. He felt like she had always been a piece of him and the thought of living only a second without her was unbearable. She looked back at him with the same intensity, the same reliance. It told him that even though she wasn't Denynso and hadn't been born with the same attachment that his kind developed for their mates, making it so that they could only ever truly love one person in their entire existence, she still felt the same level of passion and love for him.

For a third time the man appeared at the side of the table. This time he lowered a large plate to the surface between them and then slid the phone off the table back into his large hand. He walked away without acknowledging any of them and went back to his post behind the bar, wiping another glass with the cloth in his hand. Jem looked at the plate and saw it stacked with several types of food that he didn't recognize, but that Angela and Jacob grabbed up eagerly. Hunger burned in his belly and he wondered for the first time how long it had actually taken for them to transport to the museum and then escape. He picked up one of the pieces curiously and placed it in his mouth. The flavor was rich and strong, accented by something very much like the water that they drew from the purple sea on Uoria.

"Do you like it?" Angela asked with a laugh.

Jem guessed that his face expressed his surprise at the surprising flavor of the food and he nodded.

"It's different," he admitted.

They had only been eating for a few moments when the door to the bar opened and Rilex rushed in. Jem, Jacob, and

Angela jumped to their feet, surprised by his sudden appearance.

"Rilex," Jacob said. "What are you doing here?"

Jem noticed Rilex look up in the direction of the man standing behind the bar and give a slight nod. It was a gesture of acknowledgement, of familiarity. With that one gesture, the man stepped away from his post behind the bar and through a door that led deeper into the building.

"When I heard about the museum, I thought that it could be you."

"When you heard about the museum?" Angela asked.

"I have a police scanner," he said. "I like to be able to pay attention to what's going on in the area, especially with the wall here. I have to be vigilant. You never know what's going to happen – or who might show up."

There was darkness behind those words and none of them pushed him any further.

"What did you hear?" Jacob asked.

7

R ilex looked at the three faces that were staring back at him expectantly. He could barely believe that they were there. He had been trying to figure out how he was going to get in touch with them and bring them to Earth, and then the announcement came over the police scanner. It had been difficult to decipher at first. The code was complex and the voices overlapped until they were almost indivisible into words. Finally, though, he was able to figure out that it was alerting authorities to a break-in at the museum. Though they called it a break-in, the scanner specified that it was actually unauthorized people in the museum who seemed to break *out,* smashing through the front door and escaping the guard by a matter of seconds

"As soon as I heard that the people had broken through the door, I thought that it might be you," Rilex said. He gave a short laugh. "There's not many people I've ever encountered who could just smash through a door like that."

"But why did you come?" Angela asked.

"I'd been trying to find a way to get in touch with you," Rilex said. "With Jem, specifically."

Jem looked somewhat startled by the revelation.

"Me?" the warrior asked. "Why?"

Rilex felt what little amusement he had felt when thinking about Jem breaking through the glass drain away. He gestured toward the door.

"We should go."

"Go?" Angela asked. "Go where?"

"To the University. I'll explain on the way."

"The University?" Jacob asked. "That's where we were planning on going, we just didn't know how to get there. That's why we called you. We were hoping that you would be able to help us get there."

"That's where we're going," Rilex said. "I'll explain on the way."

"Wait," Angela said as they started toward the door. "The bartender. We didn't pay him for the food."

Rilex shook his head.

"It's alright," he said. "It's all settled."

He didn't go any further. That was an explanation for another time. Instead, he guided them toward the door and to where his car waited by the sidewalk. They piled in and he immediately set off toward the University. His heart was pounding in his chest as he tried to come up with the right words to say to Jem, to explain to him why he wanted to get in touch with him. Finally, he opened his mouth and simply let the words tumble out.

"I received a tip that an unauthorized shuttle appeared at the University and then another vehicle, technology that isn't recognizable, showed up as well. I have reason to believe that they are from Uoria."

"What do you mean 'unauthorized shuttle'?" Angela asked.

"The shuttle was marked for a different voyage and there

was no plan for it to return to the University at that time. The crew didn't report to the transportation department or give notice of their purpose for returning to Earth. They're currently missing."

"And the other vehicle?" Jacob asked.

"It's something that no one has ever seen. It doesn't look like any type of shuttle or ship that even the University has or is in the course of planning. It landed outside of the University laboratory building. I'm assuming it couldn't access the bay. The crew and passengers of that ship are missing as well."

"What is the University doing about them?" Angela asked. "Have they moved them?"

"No," Rilex said. "I went there before I heard the announcement over the police scanner. I wanted to see them for myself. The unknown vehicle has protective technology that prevents anyone from getting inside, but if the wrong people had access to it, I'm sure that it wouldn't last very long. I hid them to make sure that no one would be able to find them."

"How did you do that?" Jacob asked.

Rilex took a breath.

"I just did," he said. "But it's not infallible. They can't stay hidden forever, which means that we need to get there and figure out who brought them there and why before someone else does."

"Why do you think that the vehicles are from Uoria?" Jem asked.

It was the question that Rilex had known was going to come, but that he was at the most loss to answer. They were speeding toward the University and he knew that he had only limited time to explain what was happening and the urgency that he felt to get them there and figure out what was really going on.

"Since meeting you I've been devoting more of my research to Uoria and the Denynso. I wanted to understand your kind and what has been happening on the planet since first contact with the humans. I uncovered some information that might indicate that there are problems on Uoria."

"Problems?" Jem asked. "What's happening."

"I'm not absolutely sure," Rilex said. "But I feel that these vehicles have something to do with it."

"If you think that there's something wrong, why didn't you just call the University and let them know?" Angela asked. "Wouldn't they be the ones to help find the people who brought those vehicles to Earth and why?"

Rilex shook his head.

"I'm not exactly permitted to access the areas of the University that I have, and some of the research that I've been doing borders on unethical at best."

"And at worst?" Angela asked. "Illegal?"

"Deadly."

"So, you didn't call the University to protect yourself?" Jem asked, his voice angry and accusatory. "There could be countless lives at risk, but you are too afraid that you are going to get in trouble for your research that you didn't ask for help?"

"No," Rilex said. "That's not it. There are countless lives at stake *so* I didn't reach out to the University. You never know who you can trust. Sometimes the people who you think are the most on your side are actually the ones who are the most dangerous. I didn't want to risk that. I don't fully know what's happening, and I don't want to put anyone in more danger than they already are. The only one who can really help me is you."

"I don't understand why they would come without the authorization of the University," Jem said. His voice was softer now as if the anger had disappeared and given way to the fear and anxiety that he was starting to feel at the thought of his beloved home planet being in danger. "There is an alliance. There's a connection between the University and the Denynso. If my kind needed to come here for some reason, they would reach out to the representatives for the program at the University and get clearance to come."

"Maybe it doesn't have anything to do with the program," Rilex suggested.

"There's something wrong," Jem said. "The Denynso operate by duty and regulation. Laws and rules are binding. They wouldn't break the agreements made with the University lightly. Something very serious has to be happening for them to make that move."

Jem's words confirmed everything that Rilex had feared and made the urgency within him even more intense. He pushed the car faster, knowing that every single second mattered now and they needed to get to the University and to whoever was waiting there as fast as they possibly could.

Eden became aware of her heartbeat before she knew what was happening around her. Her eyelids resisted as she fought to open them, but eventually she dragged them open and was greeted by faint, hazy light. Pyra's face appeared above her and she saw a relieved smile come to his lips.

"Hey," he said. "Are you alright?"

Eden tried to sit up, but he pressed against her shoulders to ease her back down against the pile of blankets and pillows that had been propped behind her.

"Where's the baby?" she asked weakly.

"Don't try to sit up yet," Pyra said. "Ciyrs gave you something that he said would help you rest. It will probably make you a little dizzy for a while. Lysander is fine. He's with Zsilvia."

"I need to take care of him," Eden protested.

There were so many questions running through her head, but it seemed that they were so twisting and complex that she couldn't focus on them. All she could think about was Lysander and making sure that he was properly cared for.

"He's fine," Pyra said. "We changed him and I held him to you so that he could eat. Don't worry about him. You need to rest."

Eden settled back and let her body relax. She drew in and released several breaths until her heartbeat normalized and she felt the trembling from deep inside her ease.

"Where are we?" she asked.

"We're deeper in the hospital," Pyra said. "When you collapsed Ciyrs told us that we needed to get you somewhere to rest. We kept going until we found this room. Jonah says that it looks like one of the preparation chambers that used to be in hospital buildings. It seems to have served its purpose. There's bedding, clothes, emergency supplies, and even the rations are still safe after all these years. We decided to stop here for a while. We could all use something to eat and some sleep, even if it's just for a short time. We're a few floors down from the examination rooms."

Those words made a thought suddenly occur to Eden. Her eyes opened wider.

"Jonah," she said. "Where's Jonah?"

Pyra looked down at her and nodded.

"I'll get him."

A few moments later Jonah came to her side.

"Jonah," she said. "You said that the Nyx 23 mission was clandestine, and that's why each of you had to come in for your examinations separately."

The man nodded.

"Yes," he said. "Only part of the department was involved. The others didn't believe that the threat on the prison planet was enough to justify action."

"If it was a secret mission, why was there such a swift response by the Earth military?"

"What do you mean?"

"Everything I've read about the Nyx 23 mission points out that the response from the Earth military was swift and fierce. They went to the planet to try to find a trace of the crew, didn't find one, and wiped it out. That's when they named it Penthos in honor of you."

"Right," Jonah said, "but like Ryan said, that's not what really happened. The military didn't wipe out the Valdicians and free the prisoners. The general absorbed them and brought them back to Earth to use for the beginning of the breeding experiments."

"There's no memorial," she said quietly.

"What?" Jonah asked.

"No memorial," Eden repeated. "Don't you think that's strange?" They had talked about it before, but now that they were back on Earth it really sank in how out of character it was for there to be no memorial erected on Penthos for the lost team. "It is Earth's way to make memorials to honor people who have died and give others a place where they can go to pay their respects. So, an entire team goes out into the galaxy to try to fight against a rogue race that has created an illegal prison compound and goes missing, but when the military supposedly destroys the species that did it, they don't do anything?"

"What *specifically* did you learn about Nyx 23? What's in the textbooks?" Jonah asked.

"We learned that the team had identified a threat on a previously unnamed and unexplored planet. Under the belief that there was an illegal prison compound operated by a non-ally species, a small team set out on a mission with the goal of freeing the prisoners and pushing the enemies back. Mission control lost contact with the team and they didn't return as planned. A second team was then sent to the planet in an effort to find the team and understand what happened, but when they arrived they only found the prison and the enemies. There was no sign of the team. War units were deployed and the compound was destroyed. That's when they named the planet Penthos. The Nyx 23 team became martyrs, a symbol of devotion and the ultimate commitment to the quest for understanding, knowledge, justice, and protection."

"But there was never a memorial set up there? Nothing that our families could visit? Nothing even for the prisoners?"

"No," Eden said.

"Wait," Jonah said, his eyes widening slightly. "Ryan said that the general of the Earth military, his ancestor, teamed up with the Valdicians to start the breeding experiments. They were in on it."

"Yes," Eden said. "They shared the desire to breed the ultimate military force made up of hybrids, bred for their different powers and characteristics."

"So why did we end up on Uoria?" he asked.

"What do you mean?"

"Why did we end up on Uoria?" Jonah repeated. "The

Valdicians supposedly aligned with the Covra and sent us to Uoria after we raided the planet so that they could enslave us and use us in their plan to take over the Universe."

"Right," Eden said. "They had already sabotaged your ship and sent you to Uoria before the military units arrived on Penthos, though. They wouldn't have had any way of knowing that the war units would come and they would decide to go to Earth to participate in the breeding experiments."

"They wouldn't?" Jonah asked. "If they suddenly decided that they were going to go to Earth and start these complex experiments that they didn't want anyone to know about, don't you think that they would have mentioned to their new Earth allies that they had sent this mysteriously missing crew to another planet?"

"Why would they do that? Maybe they just figured that it didn't matter anymore and that they had a new venture."

"Three groups planning on taking over the Universe at the same time, specifically through the use of slaves curated from other planets and other species that have characteristics and abilities that the others don't. But they don't have anything to do with each other? Doesn't that strike you as a bit too coincidental?"

"The Covra," Eden said, her mind seeming to clear. "They wouldn't just let it go. If the Valdicians had made an agreement with them and then they reneged on it, they would retaliate."

"Exactly," Jonah said. "But they didn't. They waited. Then things went wrong and our ship crashed in the wrong place on the planet. Even then, the Covra didn't turn against the Valdicians. They waited for another generation to come so that they could continue the plan that had been put into place."

"It was designed that way," Eden said. "The entire thing. You were meant to go to the planet and confront the Valdicians. It wasn't a fluke. They didn't suddenly decide to send you to Uoria. It was all by design."

Jonah nodded.

"But whose?" he asked. "And why was my file still in that room?"

8

——————

Oro stepped through the narrow doorway into the second preparation chamber and looked around. His eyes finally fell on the faint, almost imperceptible glow that was coming from one far corner and he moved toward it.

"Ariella?" he said gently.

The glow flickered slightly and he moved closer to his mate. She was crouched against the wall, her knees pulled up to her chest and her wings tucked in against her sides. The glittering light that emanated from her was weak, tremulous as if expressing the thoughts and emotions that she was going through. The warrior lowered himself to the floor beside her and rested his back against the wall. For a few moments, he simply sat with her, allowing his presence to give her strength and reassure her that she was safe. He knew that he would do absolutely anything to protect and take care of her. His own safety wasn't even on his mind. What mattered to him was guarding his mate and fulfilling his duty to his kind.

"How will we get out of here, Oro?" Ariella asked quietly.

"We will," Oro assured her.

Ariella looked at him, staring directly into his eyes.

"You really believe that," she said.

It wasn't a question. It was a statement, an acknowledgement of the emotions that she could feel coming from him. Oro nodded and brought his hand up to tenderly cup the side of Ariella's face. She was so beautiful. She was delicate and ethereal, softer than any woman he had ever seen. He had known from the moment that he saw her that she was crafted to be his mate. It was an honor to have been granted a mate so lovely, and he knew that he would spend his life devoted to giving her all the love, passion, and protection that she deserved.

The warrior leaned down and rested his lips to hers. It was a tender kiss at first, soft and reassuring. Soon, though, Oro felt Ariella's mouth press to his more insistently. Her lips parted and the tip of her tongue touched his, seeking hungrily. He responded in kind, giving over to the need that built within him every time that he was near her. The shimmering glow around Ariella strengthened the deeper that he kissed her, and Oro tucked an arm around her waist so that he could sweep her up and onto his lap. As soon as she settled onto his hips, Oro could feel his body respond to her powerfully. She rolled her hips subtly and the growing warmth of her core nestled against his already hardening erection.

Their bodies spoke to each other without their lips ever having to say a single word. They reached out to each other through the fear and uncertainty that surrounded them and urged them to find comfort and security in each other. Oro felt Ariella's soft, fragile hands come to the front of his shirt and dip into the gap at the neckline. Just the hint of their skin touching each other was enough to push him nearly to the edge of his control, but Oro didn't want to rush. He didn't want these moments to go past him too quickly. He wanted to savor every touch of her skin, taste of her mouth, and sound of her breath rushing through her plush lips.

Oro swept his hands lightly over her breasts and then ran them around her waist until they reached the tie of her dress just beneath her wings. Tucked defensively against her sides when he first saw her, they were now standing out from her back, their glow brighter and the shimmer more visible. Oro released the tie of her dress and eased the fabric down her ribs until it pooled at her hips. He groaned softly and lowered his mouth to one of the taut pink peaks of her breasts. Her skin felt cool and velvety against his tongue and he indulged himself by swirling the tip around her nipple until he felt it harden even further. His hand came up to cup around the other and knead into the flesh, the pad of his thumb nurturing her other nipple. Ariella's gentle whimpers made everything else around him disappear and Oro felt thirsty for more of the sound. He brought his hands down to her hips and gripped their full, feminine swells. Applying gentle pressure, he guided her up to her feet so that he could ease her dress the rest of the way off.

The angle granted him perfect access to her core and he could smell the warmth of her desire for him. Oro helped her step out of the dress and tossed it aside, then gripped the back of her thighs and led her slightly forward so that she stood straddling his stomach. He kissed her belly, running his tongue along her skin briefly before lifting his head and blowing a stream of cool air along the newly dampened path. Ariella's fingers buried themselves in his thick white hair and he felt them tenderly pulling as if guiding him down. Oro happily took the invitation and continue the path of his kisses down through the valley between her hipbones and toward the downy apex of her thighs.

When he reached his destination, Oro hungrily lapped his tongue through her folds. Ariella's grip on his hair tightened and she arched her back toward him. Oro drew his tongue through her again, then slid his hands up the backs of her thighs to the juncture between her legs and hips. This new positioning of his grip allowed him to use the pads of his thumbs to carefully part the wet petals of her core to reveal the tightened peak he had coaxed forward. Oro swept the broad portion of his tongue along the vulnerable pearl and then concentrated the very tip on it until he could feel Ariella's body trembling and shaking beneath his hands.

The sound of her whimpers told Oro that she was struggling to muffle the sound, trying not to allow the others to hear them. He continued to urge her forward, swirling and flicking his tongue masterfully. As she moaned deep in her chest, Oro moved one of his hands away from her hips to untie the cords at the front of his pants. He needed to release the surging erection that was pressing almost painfully against the fabric. His cock sprung out of his pants and Oro wrapped his hand around it. Slick fluid was already forming at the tip, but it wasn't enough for him. Closing his mouth over her clit to suck it between his lips, Oro dipped his fingers into her. Gathering the hot, silky fluid onto his fingers, he brought them back to his cock and rubbed it into his skin. He wrapped his hand back around his shaft and began to stroke, mimicking the movements of his mouth on her with his hand on himself.

Suddenly Ariella let out a cry and her knees buckled. Oro caught her and eased her gently down so that she rested on his legs again. The rosy flush across her chest and the brightness in her eyes made her even more beautiful and Oro felt an even greater need for her. Fortunately, it didn't seem that Ariella was close to wanting their interaction to end. The smile on her lips balanced somewhere between satisfaction and desire, and before her breath had even fully slowed again she was walking backwards on her knees so that she straddled his legs. She leaned forward to dip her fingers into the waistband of his pants and started to pull them down. Oro lifted his hips to help her and soon the garment joined her dress on the floor beside them. He stripped away his shirt, not wanting any fabric to separate their skin.

Ariella ran her fingertips reverently along the length of Oro's cock before dipped her head down to swirl her tongue around its crown in much the same way that he had worshipped her. The sensation was almost too much for him to handle. He closed his eyes and struggled to maintain his control. He didn't want to give himself over to the climax that was already rushing toward him. He needed more time. He needed to stay longer in the pure bliss that Ariella created.

Her hot, velvety mouth slipped around Oro's erection and Ariella sucked it tenderly, bringing the tip ever closer to her throat. Her hand cupped the base of his cock and her fingers massaged deeply into the hidden bundle of nerves there. Ariella seemed to know exactly what Oro was feeling at every moment and just as he was nearing the point when he wouldn't be able to control himself any longer, she removed her mouth from him and held his erection tightly to give him a few moments to cool and calm down. His body had just begun to relax and move back from the edge of oblivion when he felt her moving back up his legs. Oro opened his eyes and watched as Ariella lifted her hips up and positioned the tip of his cock at her still-wet opening.

Oro reached between them to take his shaft in his own hand, easing hers out of the way. Flattening his other hand on her lower back, Oro made tight circles with his sensitive head into the heat of her core. Ariella's breaths deepened and her hips started to move. Finally, he rested at her opening and allowed Ariella to sink down onto his lap, enveloping him completely in her tight, hot body. They both released groans of fulfillment as their bodies melded. It was a sense of completion like nothing else in Oro's life could create. He sat up from the wall and gathered Ariella into his arms. Her skin was smooth and slick with sweat and he could feel the quickening rhythm of her heartbeat reaching out toward his through his chest.

Ariella's hips rocked to move him within her body in deep, tight strokes and Oro lifted his hips to meet them. Powerful desire swept over Oro and he lifted himself up, taking Ariella with him as he repositioned himself onto his knees and then toppled her backwards. Ariella reached back and caught herself so that she reclined back with her knees up and her body open to him. Oro pushed forward over her so that he could capture her mouth with his again. Her legs parted further, sending him driving even deeper into her. He increased his pace so that each intense thrust seemed to correspond with his heartbeat. The sensations within him were spiraling out of control and he couldn't hold himself back any longer.

Each drive of his hips brought another deep grunt from Oro's chest. He heard Ariella's gasps getting higher and faster, telling him that she was quickly moving toward another climax. Just as she cried out, her body clenching down onto his in an intense, body-trembling spasm, Oro tore his mouth away from hers and let out a roar as his own body tightened and then released into her. Ariella frantically searched for his mouth and he gave himself into her kiss as each pulse of his cock met her delicious embrace.

Their bodies were starting to relax, cooling together and seeming to meld even closer, when Oro heard Pyra's voice bellowing from the other chamber.

"Everyone eat and get as much rest as you can. We'll move out soon. If you hear anything, let me know immediately."

Oro touched another kiss to Ariella's lips and rested his forehead to hers.

"We should get some sleep," he said. "It's been a long day and we don't know what tomorrow is going to bring."

Ariella nodded.

"I feel like I can sleep better now," she whispered.

Oro laughed softly and kissed her a final time before reluctantly withdrawing from her body. They dressed and walked hand-in-hand back toward the other chamber. Though he would have preferred to have curled up with her in the privacy of the other chamber and enjoy the warmth and bond that their bodies had created, he knew that the entire group was safer if they stayed together. They walked into the main chamber and saw the others spread out across the floor, some sleeping on the thick mats they had found rolled in one corner, others eating from the bags and canisters that held food crafted specifically to last nearly indefinitely in preparation for some unknown emergency. Pyra was sitting beside Eden, who cradled Lysander in her arms as she dozed with her head back against the wall.

"Close the door, Oro," the head Denynso warrior said. "All of us are here now and we'll be safer for the next few hours if we're closed in here."

"Not all of us," Gyyx said from the other corner of the room.

Oro looked toward him and saw the desolate look in the warrior's orange eyes.

"What do you mean, Gyyx?" Pyra asked. "Who's not here?"

"Leia," he said, naming his mate. "Zuri, Samira... except for Eden, Elianna and Ariella, the women went back to Zuri's house when we came here."

"They're safe there, Gyyx," Pyra tried to reassure the warrior.

"Are they?" he asked. "We don't know where Ryan or his soldiers are. If they could find the wedding, they can find them. We're hiding down here sleeping and eating, and they could be completely at his mercy."

Oro pulled Ariella closer against his body and touched a kiss to her hair, relieved that his mate was right beside him.

"We have to be strong to survive," Pyra said. "This isn't like any battle that we have ever fought, and not all of us are accustomed to what the Denynso go through. We eat, we sleep, and then we move on. It's the only way that we are going to be able to get out of here alive, and that is the first step before we can get to the women and then to the others."

Gyyx didn't seem fully satisfied by the response, but he fell silent and Oro could see him lean back onto the pillow behind him and close his eyes. He couldn't tell if he was truly sleeping or if he just wanted to be left alone until they moved on.

9

———

Kyven felt as though they had been walking for hours, but when he glanced back over his shoulder he could still see the dark outline of the quarry behind them. He could feel Maxim and Lynx on either side of him, supporting him as he struggled to make his way across the sand. When they first dragged him and Emerie from beneath the ground he hadn't thought that his injuries were so severe, but now that the adrenaline of their escape had eased away and they were traveling back toward the ship, he could feel the pain more intensely and the weakness caused by his blood loss seemed to be dragging him down harder with each step. He fought to keep himself on his feet and not to show on his face what he was going through. He needed to remain strong for Emerie and not allow his own suffering to frighten her.

His mate had been so brave in their time trapped in the cavern beneath the rocks of the quarry. The thought of the word brought the hint of a smile to Kyven's lips. It wasn't a term that the Mikana usually used, and the fact that his mind had immediately gone to it when he thought of

Emerie made him realize just how much his time with the Denynso had influenced him. It wasn't a negative feeling, but rather one of comfort and security, as if they were finally achieving the goals that their kinds had had for their alliances generations ago and truly coming together to defend themselves, their planet, and each other.

"Can you make it?" Maxim asked quietly.

Kyven looked to his brother and nodded.

"I'm going to be fine," he said.

"Yes, you are," Maxim replied. "We're going to get you back to the ship and fix you up. We have all of the supplies from Ciyrs there and we'll be able to heal these wounds before you know it."

It was one of the few times in his life that Kyven could remember his older brother actually sounding afraid. He had always been the stronger, more positive of the two. Even when their father had died and they were suddenly thrown into a life of confusion and loss, with just their mother, Maxim had been the one that ensure that they carried through. Though Kyven didn't have as many memories of Aegeus as Maxim did because he was far younger when he left, he still carried the love and respect for him that he always had, and treasured the thoughts of his father that he maintained. Often when he looked at Maxim he was able to see Aegeus in him. He could see him in his eyes and in the occasional expression that crossed his face. There was a presence there that kept Aegeus alive with every one of Maxim's heartbeats, and sometimes it was almost as though they had melded to the point that Maxim had taken Aegeus's place.

As soon as the thought crossed Kyven's mind, he felt a shock through his heart. He remembered that his father *was* alive. At least he had been when Ryan talked to them through the screen on the ship. The thought was as startling and disquieting as it was exciting. He couldn't imagine what Aegeus had been put through in the years since he had been gone and wondered what he would be like, if he was able to see him again. Would he be the same, or would the years of torture and captivity that he had suffered through have irrevocably changed him? Would he even remember his sons or his wife, and want to be a part of their family again?

He shook his head, trying to free himself of the bitterness that was beginning to creep into his thoughts. They would only weaken him further and slow him down, and they couldn't afford to be out in the desert for even a moment longer than they had to be. Night had fallen deeply now and he could almost feel the energy of the hybrids on the planet increasing.

"What's wrong?" Maxim asked. "Do you need to stop?"

Kyven shook his head again, forcing a smile this time in an effort to tell his brother that he could keep going.

"No," he said. "I was just thinking."

"About what?"

"Papa," he admitted.

Maxim nodded and lifted Kyven a little higher, as if the mention of their father had somehow given him greater strength and endurance to keep them moving across the desert planet back toward their ship.

"He's alive," he said. "It's a miracle."

"Another miracle," Emerie murmured from behind him.

"What does she mean?" Lynx asked.

Kyven didn't know if he should tell them about Mhavyrch. The man had stayed in the cavern with them only long enough to rescue them from the creature that lurked beneath and threatened to devour them when their light failed. He had only fought off the creature enough for them to get back in control and given them the light that they needed to keep the animal at bay before disappearing back out of the cavern and into the night. It was obvious that he had been a hybrid. His appearance showed characteristics of both Denynso and Mikana along with something else that he couldn't quite identify. It didn't make sense, though. If that man had been a hybrid, that meant that he had been sent to Penthos by Ryan. He was a member of the army bred and built specifically for the purpose of destruction, and put on the mission of eliminating Maxim and him. Why would he have climbed down into the cavern to rescue Kyven and Emerie rather than killing them, or just allowing the creature to tear them apart?

He suddenly remembered some of the few words that the man had said to them.

No one deserves to die alone in the dark.

"We're alive," Kyven said.

"It seems like that might be just barely," Zyyr said. "What was that thing that was underground with you?"

Meldor, he said to himself, remembering what Mhavyrch had called the creature. It was a word that he had never heard before and one that he would never forget.

"I don't know," Kyven said. "We couldn't see it."

"You couldn't see it?" Maxim asked.

"No," Emerie said. "It would only get near us when the light was gone. If we stayed in the light, it wouldn't get close to us. We never got a chance to see it."

"I know that it was huge," Kyven said. "We could hear it breathing and I could feel it's size when it attacked us. It had thick fur, sharp claws, and fangs. It was bigger than anything that I've ever encountered."

"Have you ever heard of anything like that, Maxim?" Lynx asked.

Maxim shook his head.

"No," Maxim said. "That doesn't sound like anything that lives near the Mikana."

"Emerie?" Lynx asked. "Is that something that might come from Earth?"

"I don't know," Emerie said. "It didn't seem like anything that I know. It was too big, and the fangs and claws were too sharp."

There were a few long seconds of silence as it seemed that each of them sank away into their own thoughts. Finally, Lynx spoke up, expressing something that had briefly crossed through Kyven's mind.

"Do you think that it could be one of the hybrids?" he asked.

Kyven hissed as a sharper pain shot through the wounds on his back and he felt his body crumple toward the ground. There was something more than just the cuts in his skin that was affecting him, but he didn't know what it could be.

"Put him down," Maxim said. "We need to check his wounds again."

"Not out here," Kyven said. He was desperate for the group to get back to the ship. "You can't all put yourself in danger because of me. Get me back to the ship and then check me over."

"No," Maxim said. "There's something wrong. If we don't figure out what it is, we might not have the chance to get you back to the ship."

Kyven felt the men lower him to the sand and begin to pull at his bandages to reveal his wounds.

"There's toxin in the wounds," Lynx said. "The creature must have it in its fangs."

"What will the toxin do?" Maxim asked. "Is he going to be able to recover from it?"

"I don't know what the creature is," Lynx said, "and I don't know any more about toxins than the little bit that I picked up from Ciyrs. He taught you more about his ointments than me."

The warrior's voice was tense, but it seemed to come more from helplessness than it did anger. Emerie came to kneel beside him and rested his head in her lap. He gazed up at her as the men moved his body around, trying not to focus on the pain that was tearing through him and the burning feeling in his blood. It was dizzying and with every moment he felt like he was being dragged further and further away from this moment. He knew that he had to fight to keep himself aware and awake while the other men continued to work on him.

"I don't think that it is one of the hybrids," he said, not really directing it to any of them in particular but needing to keep words coming out of him so that he didn't allow the black cloud that was creeping into the edges of his mind to take over. "I think that it was an animal that is native to Penthos."

"Why?" Emerie asked. "Why couldn't it be one of the hybrids?"

"None of us can think of any animals that could have been combined to make something like that," Kyven said.

"That doesn't necessarily mean that it couldn't be a hybrid," Lynx said. "We don't know what kind of creatures Ryan has access to."

"No," Maxim said. "That's not why. Ryan created the hybrids with the specific purpose of turning them into an army. He chose the species that he did because of their characteristics and their ability to fight. That creature wouldn't be able to fight."

"He's right," Kyven said, his eyes closed against the pain

now. "Ryan wants hybrids that can stand up against us. That creature wasn't able to go into the light, which means that he is only effective underground or at night. I don't think that Ryan would see any purpose in breeding something with such limited effect, especially since he would have to figure out how to keep it alive"

"I don't think that he cares if any of the hybrids live," Emerie said. "They're disposable to him. They're weapons, nothing more. He doesn't care what he created or if it is destroyed."

The tone of her voice was nearly as soft as the touch of her fingertips on his cheek and held meaning that Kyven didn't want to dwell on any longer, even though he could feel it beginning within him as well. Ryan didn't care about any type of life...but did the hybrids?

10

———

"I need to know what you've found out about Uoria," Jem said.

The warrior was trying to control the aggression that was building through him. It was a feeling that he hadn't experienced since he had been on Uoria. This was the feeling of impending battle, the fury and energy of a coming war. He knew that he had to keep it tampered or his warrior training would take over, making him incredibly dangerous to anyone he might encounter.

"I can't be sure about any of it," Rilex said. "These are just rumors, it is just hints that I've gotten that have led me down different paths in my research. I don't even know what it all means."

Despite the caution, Jem knew that if the information that Rilex had gathered didn't seem compelling, he wouldn't have acted as swiftly and insistently as he had. He had uncovered something that had made him feel concerned enough that he went to find Jem, and the warrior needed to know what that was. If his kind or his planet was in trouble, it was his responsibility, his duty to help them.

"What do you know about a woman named Eden?" Rilex asked.

Jem felt the nervousness inside him spike.

"I know her well," he said. "She came to Uoria as a researcher, but she ended up staying with us. She is the mate of the Denynso leader, Pyra. She was pregnant when I left."

"Pregnant?" Rilex asked.

"Yes. The first baby of the new generation of Denynso."

There was a pause and the tension in the car seemed to increase. Rilex seemed unnerved by his response, but wasn't offering anything more about it.

"Do you know about her boss, Ryan?"

"He was the man who she was working for when she came to Uoria. He's a scientist at the University."

"Yes," Rilex said. "But do you know why he specifically sent Eden to Uoria?" he asked.

Jem felt like the man was playing some sort of game and he didn't like it. He wanted him to just be straightforward and tell him what was happening. At the same moment, though, he felt that even Rilex himself wasn't entirely sure of what he knew and was using Jem's responses to try to confirm what he was thinking. He was piecing things together as he spoke and trying to ensure that he didn't incite Jem needlessly.

"She was the first of the people in the exchange program. She came to research the Denynso and to teach us about the ways of Earth. The goal of the program is to foster relationships between Earth and the Denynso and form lines of communication and alliance."

"He could have sent any of the people from the department. Why Eden?"

"She says that she was his assistant. She worked with him on all of his projects."

"And rumor has it that she rejected his thoughts of making their relationship more than just the professional one that they already had."

Jem felt himself bristle. He remembered Eden talking about the advances that Ryan had made toward her and how they had made her feel. It disgusted him that someone would treat her that way and it felt disrespectful toward her mate that he would acknowledge it.

"Yes," he said through gritted teeth.

"Did you know that she came to Uoria with more of a purpose than just learning about the Denynso?"

"I don't understand."

"Ryan sent her to steal some of Pyra's blood."

The revelation was horrifying. It wasn't something that Pyra or Eden had ever shared with him and the thought of her being sent into that mission made his head spin. To steal a Denynso's blood was to break the oldest and most revered of Denynso laws.

"If she had tried, she would have been killed."

"Exactly," Rilex said. "From what I understand, that was why Ryan chose her. If she could be successful, he would have the most powerful blood in the universe and be able to use it for his experiments. If she wasn't, she would suffer and he wouldn't have to deal with the embarrassment and frustration of her rejection anymore."

"He wanted to kill her just because she wouldn't go along with his advances?" Jem asked incredulously.

"Partially," Rilex admitted, "but I don't think that's it. I think that he wasn't forthright about the experiments that he was doing and that she was close to figuring it out. He wanted to eliminate the threat to his work."

"But she didn't die and she didn't bring him Pyra's blood. She joined the clan," Jem said.

"Exactly. What happened to the other women from the program?"

"They joined the clan as well," Jem said. "They bonded with other Denynso. I don't understand what any of this has to do with the problems that you said that you think are happening on Uoria."

"I think that Ryan's experiments are far more dangerous than anyone knew. Sending Eden to Uoria was just one piece of a plan that is in motion, and that's why people from Uoria are at the University. They were brought there for a reason."

"Why?" Jem asked.

"I'm not sure, but honestly I don't think that I want to know. We just need to get there as fast as we can."

The distance between the bar and the University seemed to stretch further and further with each moment, but finally Jem saw imposing buildings rising on the horizon in the distance. Lights positioned along their edges and along the perimeter of the complex made their silhouettes stand out starkly and Jem wondered which of them was the laboratory. Rilex pulled the car up to a massive gate and reached out to press a small piece of metal onto a screen positioned at the top of a pole at the edge of the road.

"Where did you get that?" Angela asked from beside Jem.

"What was it?" Jem asked.

"An access chip," Angela said. "Only people authorized to enter the University complex are supposed to have one."

"I stole it," Rilex said.

"What?" Angela asked, sounding shocked.

"I didn't have a choice," Rilex said. "When I came

through the portal, I didn't have anything and had no idea where I was. I had to create a life that was believable, and part of that meant that I had to steal parts of other people's lives. When this system was first implemented, I stole a chip so that I would be able to access the University if I thought that it might help me."

"If one of those chips is necessary to get into the gate to the complex, how did the unauthorized vehicle get in?" Jem asked.

"I don't know," Rilex said. "That's another reason that I have to believe that that vehicle didn't come from Earth. Either someone on it had an access chip or the vehicle is capable of utilizing the sky corridors like the shuttles, but didn't have access to the bay and was able to land on the grounds. Like I said, it's not technology that I've ever seen."

Rilex directed the vehicle along a road that circled around toward the back of the complex. They traveled past countless buildings and Jem found himself getting over-whelmed by the sheer volume of the space and the towering structures that seemed to bear down on him.

"How are we going to find them?" Jem said. "If that shuttle and vehicle are from Uoria, how are we going to find whoever was on them in all these buildings?"

"Ryan only works in the laboratory building," Rilex explained. "That's that tall building up ahead. All of the University's research and experimental laboratories are in that building. He doesn't have access to the other buildings except for the main administrative building, but there would be little benefit to him there. If he's doing experi-ments, no matter what kind they are, he would be doing them in the laboratory building."

"But wouldn't that mean that anyone in the building would find them?" Angela asked.

"Not necessarily," Rilex said. "Just like the access chips control movement in and out of the complex, there are controls in place in the building to keep people in the areas where they are authorized. That would put some level of protection for him. But I don't think that's it."

"What do you mean?" Jacob asked.

"Do you know how long this complex has been here?" Rilex asked.

"The buildings?" Jacob asked. "About a hundred years. It's the oldest standing University. There've been upgrades, but the structures themselves were built about a century ago."

"Not the buildings," Rilex said. "The complex."

"It was here for probably just as long before that. Maybe even longer," Angela said. "They closed the entire thing in phases, demolished it, and rebuilt."

"Right," Rilex said. "Only one portion took much longer to rebuild than the others."

"The laboratory building," Jem said.

Rilex stopped the car and reached into the glove compartment. He drew out a screen and input commands until what looked like a set of building plans appeared on it.

"These are the old buildings," he said. "You can see that they are laid out completely differently than the new University. Their laboratory building was on the complete opposite side of the complex. When they rebuilt the new laboratory, someone decided to move it, and then put it here."

He pointed to the screen and Jem looked at the word beside where his finger sat.

"Hospital?" he asked.

Rilex nodded.

"Look at these plans," he said, changing the screen to a

different set. These looked more basic, as if only showing the structure of each of the planned buildings. "What do you notice about the laboratory building?"

Jem looked at the plans, trying to understand what Rilex was trying to get him to see. Suddenly it struck him.

"It's smaller," he said.

"Exactly," Rilex said. "The original plans for the laboratory only had it as ten stories. Look at the current building."

Jem looked back up at the tall building ahead of them.

"Twelve," Angela said.

"And the hospital?" Rilex said, switching back to the other plans.

"Two," Jacob said.

"Right," Rilex said. "There was a floor of examination rooms and a floor of inpatient rooms. The surgical suites were underground."

"I've been in that building, though," Jacob said. "The first floor is all offices. The next two are student labs. There isn't a hospital."

"So, you've been to the third floor?" Rilex asked.

"Yes."

"Was it as deep as the first two?"

"What do you mean?"

"What was in the back of the building?"

"Staircases."

"Did they line up to the ones on the first two floors?"

"No," Jacob said. "It was built with extra space on the upper floors to give the researchers more room in their laboratories and offices."

"But the bottom floors are the same size from the outside," Angela said softly as if something was coming together in her mind.

"So, what's in that space?" Jem asked.

"There are no doors on either of the first two floors that lead into the surplus space. On the modified plans, the area is marked as being solid. The official explanation is that they wanted extra support for the laboratories and to make the building itself more stable."

"That doesn't make any sense," Angela said."

Rilex shook his head.

"No, it doesn't."

"That's where they are," Jem said.

"It's a start," Rilex agreed. "We just have to figure out how to get in."

11

———

"Are you sure that you want to come?" Samira asked, looking into the rearview mirror to where her mother sat in the backseat.

Valerie didn't hesitate before nodding.

"Absolutely," she said. "You and these people who you brought here rescued me. I'm not going to turn my back on them if I have the chance to do something for them."

Samira's heart swelled and she felt tears building in her eyes. Her mother had changed so much in just the brief time since she had walked away from Samira's stepfather. Valerie suddenly looked alive. Her eyes were bright and clear for the first time in as long as Samira could remember. She no longer held the expression of fear and exhaustion that always seemed etched on her face, and she was finally holding her shoulders straight rather than sagging down like she was trying to make herself as small and unnoticeable as she could be. It made Samira feel proud to see how much Valerie had improved, and gave her a sense of joy that it seemed her mother was finally coming out of the darkness that her husband had put her in and was going to take hold of her own life again. Samira would never be able to express enough gratitude to Ero for what he had done for her. In his first visit to Earth, when he had come for Zuri, he had gone to Valerie's home and confronted Samira's stepfather. It was that moment that had begun the change in Valerie's life.

"Have you been able to contact Gyyx, Leia?" Zuri asked.

Samira saw Leia shake her head. The small woman looked even more fragile than she usually did as she stared out of the car window into the darkness of the night beyond. She hadn't been able to reach out to her mate since they had escaped the wedding and she had become progressively weaker and quieter. Zuri drew in a breath.

"I haven't been able to get in touch with Ero, either," Zuri said.

"What do they mean?" Valerie asked.

"Usually the Denynso can communicate with their mates through their thoughts. It lets them speak to us without having to say something out loud, or communicate when we aren't together. None of us have been able to connect with our mates, though. They've blocked their minds," Samira said. "They're preventing communication with us."

"Why would they do that?" Valerie asked.

"There has to be a reason," Zuri said. "I know that there have been times when the warriors have blocked their communication during battles or other particularly stressful times. They don't want us to be able to sense what is going on with them."

"That's what I'm afraid of," Leia said softly. "I'm scared that they are in danger. They've been gone for too long. They should have come back by now. We should have gone to them sooner."

"They told us to stay at the house," Samira said. "They said it was too dangerous for us to go with them."

"Why did Elianna go?" Leia asked. "Eden's there. Zsilvia is there."

"Zsilvia was there before the Valdicians got to the wedding, which means that is it very likely she was captured. Eden went because it was her child that was taken. There's nothing that would keep a mother from her child in that situation and she too is a healer. And you know why Elianna is there," Samira said.

She didn't want to say it. She didn't want to put voice to the fear that was threatening to take over her thoughts and control her, distracting her from driving. Each of the women who had lived among the Denynso knew of the unique skill that Elianna had. Her arrival on Uoria had been extremely difficult and she nearly died after an attack, putting her in Ciyrs's clinic for days. The healer had put everything into healing her and though he was finally successful, she had not come out of the healing unchanged. During the course of the healing Ciyrs had transferred some of his healing capabilities to her, giving her the ability to heal injuries and illnesses, and imbuing her with much of his knowledge of the plants, ointments, and powders that could be used to further heal those who needed it. When Eden and the men had left for the lab to confront Ryan, Elianna went along in anticipation of violence. If any of their group was injured, having three healers would improve the chances that they would be able to get them out and back to safety.

"How much further?" Valerie asked.

Samira realized that her mother had never made it to the University to visit her in the entire time she had been studying there. Her stepfather had never permitted her much movement outside of the house and Valerie would never have gotten the opportunity to make the trip out just to see where Samira studied. Though she wished that it was under better circumstances, Samira was happy that Valerie was finally able to see the place that had been so important in her life up until this point. She knew in her heart that she wouldn't be returning here even after the conflict with Ryan was over. Her life was irrevocably changed by Ty and she would follow him back to Uoria.

"We're almost there," Samira told her. "Mom, please think about this. I don't know what's going on at the University or what is going to happen. I can't promise you that you are going to be safe once we get there."

"I haven't been safe since you were a little child, Samira," Valerie said. "I survived your stepfather. I'm not afraid."

The words stabbed deeply into Samira, though she knew that her mother hadn't intended them to. She knew that Valerie had suffered extensively under her stepfather's hands. She had gone through enough on her own. Now Valerie had finally gotten out from under him, but almost as soon as she had taken a breath of freedom, Samira was bringing her back into the face of unpredictable danger.

A few moments later the car pulled up to the gate at the University. She touched her access chip to the screen and the gates swung open, allowing her access. Looking around cautiously, she drove along the road toward the laboratory building. As they approached, she noticed that there was another car sitting in the small parking lot. Its appearance sent a shiver through her. She knew every vehicle of every person authorized to be inside the laboratory building, and she didn't recognize that car.

"Who is that?" Zuri asked.

"I don't know," Samira said. "Do you recognize it?"

"No," Zuri said.

They pulled up alongside the car and paused for a moment, each of them looking out of the windows to detect anyone who might still be in the area. Not seeing anyone, Samira climbed out of the car. The other women followed and Samira took her bag from Zuri, dropping it over her shoulder as she stared at the building ahead.

"Are you ready?" she asked, looking to the other women.

They all nodded at her and they started across the wide grassy expanse between the parking lot and the laboratory building. The feeling in the area was eerie. Everything was too still, too quiet. The air seemed to crackle with energy and it was getting harder to breathe with each step.

"How do we get inside?" Valerie asked in a tense whisper.

Samira looked to Zuri for guidance just as she had since she met her. Zuri scanned the area briefly.

"Let's go to the side entrance," she said. "It's less exposed than the front. There's less of a chance for anyone to see us going inside."

They picked up their speed as they moved toward the building, each one of them recognizing the urgency to get out of clear view. Samira strained for any sound to come to her over their footsteps, but there was nothing. They finally reached the building and Samira felt a strange sensation wash over her. She had taken this same path countless times before. Any other time she would have felt that she could navigate the grounds and even the building itself with her eyes closed, but now as she got closer to the entrance it felt less and less familiar. It was almost as though she didn't know where she was or where to go, as if she wasn't within her own body and was rather watching what she was doing from a distance. She strug-gled to get back in control of her emotions, to put herself back into the moment and focus on what she needed to do.

They turned the corner of the building and Samira stopped short. The other women stopped around her and she knew that they were seeing what she was. Ahead of them she could see movement in the shadows of the building. Samira stretched her arm out to block the other women from moving further. They crouched down closer to the ground, staying close to the wall. The movement in the distance divided into four distinct figures and Samira felt a sudden surge of anger. Her husband, her mate, was somewhere in this building and she needed to get to him. If these figures had anything to do with it, she wasn't going to back down.

Samira stood and stepped out of the shadow of the wall. Her focus narrowed on the figures and she started toward them. Suddenly she saw a flicker of something appear near the figures, then disappear. She took another step and it appeared again. This time it remained and she could see that it was a strange car parked close to the building. The figures stepped closer to it, moving further into the light, and she noticed that one of them looked extremely large, the size of a Denynso warrior, while the other three were smaller. They were walking around the car, examining it carefully. She wanted to call out to them, but at the same moment she didn't want to announce her presence yet.

Suddenly one of the smaller figures stepped fully into the light and Samira realized that it was a woman. As if she could feel Samira's eyes on her, the woman stopped and turned to look at her. She looked startled and stepped back against the car, reaching over the hood toward the massive figure still partially in the shadows. It stepped forward into the light and took her hand over the hood, then looked toward Samira. The impact of his gaze took Samira's breath from her chest. She felt like her legs were going to give out beneath her, but she had to keep standing to continue looking at him, to ensure that she was seeing what she thought she was. It had been so long, but she knew the curve of his face and the smile that came to his lips when he seemed to recognize her.

"Jem."

She thought that she had yelled out to him. She wanted to call out to him, but the name had come out only as a whisper. Zuri came up beside her and she felt the other woman's hand grip hers at her side. Jem came around the side of the vehicle and an instant later they were running toward each other. The warrior swept Samira into a hug and she immediately felt the intense heat coming from his skin. It wasn't as searing as it would have been if she didn't have a mate, but it was enough that she needed to step back from him. This was a protective feature embedded in the genes of the Denynso. Once one of the men found their mate, his skin became unbearably hot to the touch of any other woman. It often lessened the longer that he was bonded to his mate, which meant that Jem's bond was likely very new.

"You're alive!" she said as she stepped back from him and looked up into his smiling face. "How? How is this possible?"

"Samira, it is so good to see you. Zuri, Leia. I can't believe you're here. There's so much to tell you, and I'll explain it all, but right now we need to find the others. They need our help."

"The others?" Zuri asked. "You know that they're here?"

The three others who had been near the car with Jem came up behind him, looking at the women curiously. The younger of the two men looked slightly familiar to Samira, but she couldn't place him.

"This is Rilex," Jem said, gesturing toward the older of the men. "He told me that two unauthorized vehicles appeared here. One is a shuttle and this is the other one," he pointed toward the car. "He thinks that they're from Uoria."

"A shuttle?" Samira asked. "Another shuttle?"

"Another?" Jem asked. "What do you mean?"

"We arrived on a shuttle several days ago, but that was an authorized trip. If there is an unauthorized shuttle here, that means that others have come."

"The more of the Denynso who are here, the more danger there is," Rilex said.

"He's right," Samira said. "Ryan is luring us all here. This isn't just about Lysander."

"Lysander?" Jem asked.

Samira felt her stomach turn slightly. He hadn't been there when Pyra and Eden's baby was born. Lysander had become such an integral part of the clan as a whole that it was difficult to think of them without him, but she realized that in his mind that was the way things were. He didn't know of any of the changes that had happened on the planet or within the clan since that last battle, from the moment that he disappeared from them.

"Eden and Pyra's son," she said.

"Their son," he said with a soft smile.

Samira nodded.

"He was born a few months after you..." she paused, not knowing what to say. She was so accustomed to thinking of the moment when he threw himself into the sky in Loralia's realm as his death, but now he was standing before her and she had to change the way she thought. "After you left. Now Ryan has him."

She could see the panic rise in Jem's eyes.

"What?" he asked. "Why does Ryan have him?"

"We don't know. He sent creatures to my wedding and stole the baby."

"Your wedding."

It was another moment of painful reality.

"Ty and I got married," she told him.

"Congratulations," he said uncertainly. He reached behind him to take the hand of the woman she had first seen beside the car and guide her up to stand beside him. "This is Angela, my mate."

Samira nodded at Angela, but didn't greet her. They would have time to talk later. For now, they were letting precious moments slip away from them.

"Do you know where they are?" Samira asked. "You said Rilex knew the vehicles were here. Does he know where they've gone?"

"No," Jem said, "but he has an idea."

Samira listened as Rilex explained the plans of the building and pointed out a section that could be covering a building that had been abandoned many years before. It was something that she would never have considered, but she had no other idea. There was no other option.

"How do we get to that section of the building, though?" Samira asked.

"If it's sealed off so that none of us even knew that it existed, how would they have gotten to it?"

"I don't know," Rilex said. "We're just going to have to look."

"What about the locks?" Leia asked. "We'll only be able to access certain parts of the building using Zuri and Samira's codes."

"I'll take care of it," Rilex said. "Where are the master controls."

"They would have to be in the main administrative office," Zuri said. "But none of us have authorization to the controls."

"Just show me where to find them," he said. "I'll handle it from there."

FROM THE MOMENT that they stepped into the laboratory building, Samira felt the energy shift again. It was thicker here, more intense, and she felt like there were eyes on her from every direction. They were walking through the darkened main hallway when she heard a scuffling sound behind her. She turned and saw a shrouded figured come around the corner. Something glistened by its side and it started toward them aggressively. Jem turned and leapt at it, directing the impact of his shoulder directly into the creature's gut. There was a gasping sound as they hit the floor and Samira felt someone grab at her wrist.

"Come on," Zuri insisted. "Now!"

Jem was still thrashing on the ground with the creature but she let Zuri pull her so that they started running down the hall in the direction of the administrative office. Rilex pressed an access chip to the sensor at the side of the door and she was stunned to hear it click open. As they streamed into the office she could hear thudding footsteps behind her and when she glanced over her shoulder she was relieved to see Jem coming toward her. There was a streak of blood along his arm, but he didn't seem injured.

As if they could still feel the breath of the creature on their necks, they ran through each phase of the office until they reached a massive steel door that protected the main controls of the building. Rilex pressed his access chip to the sensor, but it didn't respond. Samira felt her stomach sink. Rilex took a breath.

"Step back," he said. "Turn your back and close your eyes."

"What are you going to do?" Samira asked.

"Please just do it," Rilex said sternly. "We don't have time for explanations."

Samira saw Jem take Angela by the hand and guide her to the other side of the room. The man who had come along with them followed and they turned their backs to Rilex without hesitation, as if they knew what he was planning on doing. Samira, Zuri, Leia, and Valeria followed and took their places beside the others. Samira felt herself drawing close to her mother, seeking out the same level of comfort that she would have when she was a small child. Valerie reached down and held her hand, squeezing it tightly. For the first time in so long, she was the strong one.

Samira closed her eyes and almost immediately heard a deafening blast from behind her accompanied by a searing light that brought her hands up to cover her closed eyes. It intensified until she thought it would burn through her and then finally darkened again. She felt breathless and it took a moment before the disorientation faded and she could move again. Turning back toward the steel door she saw that it was standing open, the sensor now melted and smoking. She ran past it into the room with the main controls and found Rilex standing over them, examining them.

"Do you know how to work them?" he asked.

Samira shook her head.

"No. Only authorized administration does."

"When I tell you to, I need you to leave the office as fast as you can. Go back out to the main hallway."

Samira nodded her agreement and Rilex returned the gesture. She watched as he reached beneath his shirt and pulled out a small pouch that was dangling from a cord around his neck. He reached into it and withdrew what looked like a tiny pebble. Rilex settled the pebble into a crevice in the main control panel, then leaned down and blew onto it.

"Go," he said.

Samira started out of the office and took only a second to glance back over her shoulder. She saw Rilex blowing on the pebble again, and where it was rested in the panel had begun to glow. The illumination began to intensify quickly and Rilex began to run toward her. They wove their way back through the office and out into the main hallway. They had just reached the body of the creature that attacked them when she heard another blast that made the building shudder and made her body feel almost liquid. Around her the air dissolved into the buzz of an alarm and a nearby panel in the wall flashed a red message.

Main Controls Deactivated. All Units Unlocked. Main Controls Deactivated. Please Utilize Alternative Security.

Whatever Rilex had done it had destroyed the main controls of the building, releasing all of the locks throughout it. They could now move through the building freely, but that still meant that they had to find their way to the abandoned section.

12

Dizziness swept over Ivy and she felt her body sway. Arms caught her and started guiding her away from the panic room and back into the main chamber of the shuttle. When she felt the soft cushion of the lounge chair beneath her she opened her eyes and saw Lila standing over her. Her cool hand brushed across Ivy's forehead and she gave a gentle, knowing smile.

"Rest," she whispered. "You have more to think about than the rest of us."

Ivy was surprised by the revelation, but she reminded herself that this woman was not only Mikana as they thought her to be when they met her in the kingdom. Instead she was a descendant of the Eteri, a beautiful and mysteriously skilled blend that allowed her to sense what was within those she came near. In that moment, she was utilizing her skill quite literally, sensing not just her, but the tiny child that she carried. She had told only Maxim, agreeing that they should wait to tell the others until after the conflict. Enough of her own thoughts and concentration were focused on her pregnancy. She knew that if she told any of the others about the baby that they, too, would worry about her and right then they needed each of them to be fully focused on the challenges that lay ahead.

"Please don't say anything," she said.

Lila shook her head.

"Of course not."

Ivy had just let out a relieved breath when Elise rushed into the chamber. Her cheeks were high with color and her fists were clenched by her side. She strode heavily across the chamber until she reached the windows and then turned back around, taking another few steps before stopping. She looked like she wanted to say something, but the fury she was feeling was preventing the words from forming. Rain quickly came in after her and rested a hand to her back.

"How could they do this?" Elise finally said. "How could they just hide?"

Ivy looked at the entrance to the kitchen but didn't see the three men who had been in the panic room.

"Where are they?" she asked. "You didn't put them back in there, did you?"

Rain shook her head.

"No. They went back to their quarters to take showers and change clothes. I don't think that they want to be seen in their uniforms right now."

"I don't blame them," Ivy said. "I will admit, though, that it disturbs me a little that there were three men onboard that we didn't even know were here. I mean, I knew that the ship had a crew when we got on it, but after we landed here, I just assumed..." her voice trailed off and she shook her head. "I don't know what I assumed. They were just gone and I didn't think about them again. Maybe part of me thought that the Valdicians had killed them."

"Like when Leia was headed to Uoria," Rain said.

Ivy nodded.

"Who's Leia?" Elise asked.

"The men in the panic room," Ivy said.

"Elon, Avery, and Michael?" Elise asked.

"Yes. One of them said that there had been a hijacking before and that's why they implemented all of the safety protocols."

"Yes," Elise said. "That was Avery, the pilot."

"Leia was on the ship that was hijacked," Ivy explained. "It was taken over by Klimnu when they were headed to Uoria. They killed the pilot and the crew and then took Leia captive. They held her in a prison on Uoria for months before Elianna discovered her and brought her back to the compound."

"So, they designed safety protocols that would protect the crew, but not the passengers?" Elise asked.

"Apparently," Rain said.

"I'm sorry." Ivy turned toward the voice and saw Avery step cautiously into the room. He was dressed in casual clothes now, but he still carried himself with the stiff formality of a pilot. "I shouldn't have gone into the panic room. The others were following my command, and I take full responsibility for it. I should have stayed out with the rest of you and faced whatever happened."

"You have no loyalty to us," Rain said. "There'd be no reason for you to do anything but exactly what you did: save yourself."

"It doesn't matter who I give my loyalty to," Avery contended. "I am the pilot of this ship and I should be the one that leads it no matter what happens."

"Maxim is our leader," Ivy said. "Even if you had stayed out, it wouldn't have changed that. You don't know what you're facing."

"You are the one who condemned us for hiding," he said, starting to sound angrier. "You pointed out that there were so many species out there right now unified and fighting, and that none of you ever hid."

"I know what I said," Ivy told him calmly, "and I know what I'm saying now. You did as you were told and that is probably the best choice to have made, even if it wasn't the courageous choice. You wouldn't have known what to do even if you had chosen to stay. You pilot pleasure cruises. This is war."

The man looked stung and he seemed to be getting ready to say something to her, but a loud knock on the door to the shuttle silenced him. His face went pale and he looked as though he wanted to run back into the panic room. Elise walked over to the door and stood close to it.

"Yes?" she called.

"Elise, it's us," Kyven's voice called from the other side of the thick metal. "Unlock the door."

Ivy turned to Rain, who nodded.

"It's them and it's safe. There isn't anyone with them."

"How does she know that?" Avery asked.

"My mate is out there with them," Rain answered. "He can communicate with me through his thoughts. No one else can hear them. If one of the hybrids had captured them and was trying to get inside with them so that they could overtake us and the ship, he would be able to tell me without them knowing and I would tell Elise to keep them doors locked. I guess you can call that *our* safety protocol."

Ivy watched as Elise input the codes to release the lock on the door and opened it. Maxim stepped in and moved out of the way to allow Zyyr inside. Kyven was draped across his shoulders and though his eyes were open, Ivy could see that the Mikana man was not well.

"What's wrong?" she asked, standing from the lounge and crossing to Maxim. "Was he hurt in the fall?"

The rest of the group came inside and Elise promptly closed the door, inputting the codes again to lock them inside.

"There was something in the quarry with them," Maxim explained. "Some kind of creature. It attacked him."

"There were toxins on its fangs or claws," Lynx said. "We tried the healing ointments that we brought with us, but it's still influencing him. It's getting stronger. We need to get the wounds completely clean and dress them again."

"Bring him to the infirmary," Avery said. "Elise, go to Elon's quarters and tell him he's needed there." Avery looked to Ivy and then at the others. "Elon is our medic. He might be of some help to you."

"We have our own methods of healing," Zyyr said protectively.

"I know," Avery said. "I respect that, and we wouldn't get in your way. But he might be of some service to you. Whatever you might need, he'll be there to help. Please. I know that we made the wrong decision when we first came here, but I'd like to show you that we want to be a part of this with you."

"You don't even know what's happening," Ivy protested.

"Ivy," Maxim said, quieting her. "He might not fully understand what's happening, but he's offering his service to us. Don't turn your back on help. Especially when we need it the most."

Ivy felt a hint of color splash across her cheeks. She knew that Maxim was right. She stepped back toward the lounge and rested onto it again, needing another moment to let the dizziness fade away again.

"I'm sorry," she said softly.

"Thank you," Maxim said, stepping toward Avery, his hand extended in the way that Ivy had taught him to greet humans.

"Avery," the pilot told him, taking his hand.

"My name is Maxim. Thank you, Avery."

Elise led Zyyr out of the room and Avery followed. Maxim watched until they were gone and then turned to Ivy. He came to the lounge chair and sat on the edge, leaning over so that he could rest his head on her chest. She cupped her hand around the back of his head and relaxed with the feeling of his breaths traveling across her skin.

"Where's Nylek?" Lila suddenly asked.

Ivy's eyes snapped open and she looked at Maxim, who had sat up sharply.

"Nylek didn't find you?" she asked.

"No," Maxim said. "He wasn't here when we left."

"He showed up just a little while later," Ivy said. "He insisted that he go to the quarry to help you. He figured that he would either get there while you were still there or he would meet you somewhere along the way. You didn't find him?"

"No," Maxim said, starting to sound nervous. "He's still out there somewhere. The hybrids might have found him by now. I have to go find him."

Maxim jumped up and Ivy reached for him, grabbing him by his wrist and trying to pull him back down to her. The thought of him going back out into the darkness was terrifying. She needed him there with her. She didn't want to be left alone in the shuttle again, pacing and waiting, helpless and ineffective.

"I can't leave him out there alone," Maxim said. "He left his mate and his home to come with us and help. We can't abandon him."

Ivy knew that he was right. Nylek was one of their number, a warrior who offered himself into service of his king even though he wasn't a part of the initial journey that had brought them there. If he was still out in the desert, he could be in serious danger, and they had to do whatever they could to return that courage. Maxim disappeared into the chambers deeper in the shuttle and came back wearing a thick cloak that he must have gotten from his pod.

"Lynx," he called. The warrior came out of the kitchen and Maxim tossed him another cloak. "Nylek is still out there. We need to go find him. Rain, could you please get Elise and ask her to unlock the door?"

"I can do it," Avery said, stepping back into the room. "Kyven is resting," he said. "He's in the infirmary and they were able to clean his wounds and apply ointments deeper in his skin. Elon put some sutures in, which should help them heal more quickly. He's resting now."

"Thank you, Avery," Maxim said.

He tightened the tie of the cloak around his neck and came back to Ivy. He stroked his fingertips along the curve of her jaw and looked into her eyes.

"I will be back as soon as I can," he said. "Go to bed. I need to know that you are safe and warm, and you need to sleep."

"Maxim," she started, but he leaned down and touched his lips to hers to quiet the words.

"I'll be back," he whispered. "Go to bed. I love you."

"I love you," Ivy whispered.

She watched as Avery went to the panel and input the code that unlocked the door. Maxim and Lynx stepped out and before they were even off the stairs, the former pilot closed the door again and locked it. He turned toward Ivy and she could see hope in his eyes. Despite Maxim's admonishment, she still couldn't bring herself to trust the man. Without saying a word to him, she stood and walked in the direction of the infirmary, hoping that she wouldn't encounter Elise along the way. She wanted to take a shower and change into fresh clothes so that she could slip into bed and drift away until Maxim was back with her.

MAXIM DROPPED to his knees in the sand beside the form lying face down beneath a long black cloak. He tucked his hand beneath the form and flipped it over, revealing Nylek's face. Lynx knelt on his other side and lifted his head, feeling his neck for a pulse.

"He's alive," he said. "Check for injuries."

Maxim ran his hands down Nylek's arm and then along his chest and stomach. He felt something cold and wet against his hand and looked down to see blood shining on his hand in the moonlight. Even with his hand rested directly on the warrior's chest Maxim could barely feel his breaths, and he knew that they needed to get him back to the shuttle immediately if they were going to have any chance of saving him. Lynx scooped Nylek into his arms and they started back to the shuttle. As they went, Maxim's mind wandered to Ivy and the baby that she was carrying. Being a father was never something that he had considered before, but now that it was happening, it felt completely natural, as though it was something that was always there but he only now discovered it. Suddenly his entire world was focused in on two heartbeats and for now those hearts beat together, ensconced within the same protective body. Someday, though, they would be separate and all his love would have to exist in two places.

By the time that they got Nylek back to the shuttle, his breathing had stopped completely. Maxim pounded on the door, calling in to Avery or Elise to let them in. As soon as the door opened, Lynx rushed Nylek to the infirmary. Maxim watched as Elon left Kyven's side and came to the bed where Lynx had placed Nylek's limp and unresponsive body. He felt a shudder deep within him as Elon cut away Nylek's clothes and reached for pieces of equipment that were attached to the wall and ceiling. He attached them to Nylek's chest and the insides of his wrists, then pressed a button. The warrior's body arched, but fell limp again. Maxim tried not to think of what happened to him when he was out in the desert, to wonder what had caused the deep gash that he could now see meandering across his stomach and up to his chest, to feel the guilt crushing down on him that Nylek had left the safety of the shuttle to come to him and he had never found him. As hard as he tried, though, Maxim couldn't push away the thought in his mind, wondering if Nylek had called out to his mate as he collapsed to the ground and lay dying in the cold.

Suddenly there was a gurgling sound from the bed and Nylek's chest expanded as he filled it with a deep breath.

"Is he going to be alright?" Maxim asked.

"That's still left to be seen," Elon said. "For now, he's breathing and his heart's beating. If I can keep him stable for a while longer, I can attempt surgery on his wound. If he survives that, his next challenge will be getting through the night. After that, he has a good chance."

Maxim nodded and stepped over to Kyven's bed. He looked down at his brother, grateful for the look of peaceful sleep on his face. His lower body was covered with a sheet, but Maxim could see that nearly his entire upper body was wrapped in tight bandages. On the edges, some of the healing ointments had soaked through, giving the pristine fabric a green cast. He knew that beneath those bandages his brother's skin had been stitched back together, a concept that was both foreign and frightening to Maxim. He couldn't stand there any longer, listening to the strange sounds coming from the equipment attached to Nylek or looking at the bandages seeming to engulf his brother. They had been on Penthos for such a short time, and already two of their own lay tattered.

Maxim backed out of the infirmary and walked to the bank of showers in the room adjacent to it. He stood under the water until he felt all the twitching, adrenaline-fueled energy stream out of his muscles. Wrapped in a towel, he left the showers and returned to the chamber where his and Ivy's pods had been for the journey. The travel pods had been converted to sleeping accommodations and in the faint glow of emergency strips along the ceiling he could see Ivy resting quietly. She had left the space beside her open for him and it was one of the most welcome sights that he had ever seen. Maxim closed the door to the chamber and let the towel drop to the floor. Lifting the edge of the blanket, he slid into the bed and let his body sink into the mattress. Though he had been as careful as he could, the movement made Ivy stir and she gave a little sigh.

Maxim slid across the mattress to her and molded his body to her back. Through the gauzy white fabric of her nightgown he could feel the warm of her skin and it took away the deep chill that even the shower hadn't been able to remove. Ivy smelled sweet and clean and her skin felt soft as he ran his fingertips along her arm. Ivy sighed again at his touch and her back arched as she pressed her hips back against his. Maxim touched a kiss to her shoulder and returned the pressure of her hips. After a moment, Ivy rolled over onto her back and her eyes opened to look at him. She gave a sleepy smile and Maxim dipped his head to brush his mouth across it. Ivy caught his lips in hers and he felt her hands come to his back. The gentle pressure of her touch guided him over so that he lay on top of her and their kiss deepened. There was nothing urgent in the way that their mouths moved across each other. It was only calm, nurturing tenderness that reassured each that the other was there.

Ivy reached down and took hold of her nightgown, easing it up her thighs and over her hips. Maxim lifted his chest off her to allow her to remove it the rest of the way, and then settled back down onto her. The warmth of their skin touched from shoulder to their tangled feet and everything else fell away. Nothing else mattered but the rise and fall of her breasts against his chest and the fullness of her lips beneath his mouth as her hands ran languidly along his back. He craved her. Not in a way that was harsh or aggressive, but in the way that she filled him, satisfied him, and breathed life back into him when he felt that it was draining out of him.

One hand trailed along her side, feeling the ridges of her ribs and then the deep dip of her waist before the lush swell of her hip. He continued the touch down to her thigh and guided her leg up to his bend beside his hip. The movement opened her body to him and Maxim could feel the heat of her waiting core against his already hardened erection. Ivy moved her other leg out slightly to open further and Maxim felt his tip press into her opening. She sighed at the touch and Maxim lifted up slightly to sink the rest of the way into her. Her body molded around his perfectly and he paused deeply within her just to enjoy the way that it felt to have the embrace of her walls around him. He kissed along the side of her neck, creating a slow, gentle trail down to her collarbone where he let the tip of his tongue glide out against her skin.

When he finally began to move his hips, it was in long, unhurried strokes that ensured she could feel him touch every inch within her. The desperate need he had for her was nearly overwhelming. Watching Kyven and Nylek both nearly slip away had only solidified how precious she was to him and how vital to his life she truly was. Ivy was his breath and his blood, his reality and his dreams. Without her he knew that he could do nothing, and with her he was willing to endure anything.

There was nothing frantic or rushed in the way that his body delved into hers, but soon he could feel himself nearing climax. Pressure built throughout his body, fueling him to press slightly deeper and harder with each stroke until finally it broke and he felt everything within him pour out into her. Maxim rose up a few inches and ran his hand down her belly until he could press the pad of his thumb against her peak. He massaged it in tight, hard circles as he leaned down to draw one of her nipples in between his lips and suck it gently. It took only a few moments of this attention for her to let out a gasping cry as Maxim felt her body close tightly around him and draw him deeper with a series of intense spasms.

Maxim lowered himself carefully down onto Ivy and then rolled to the side, scooping her up against him so that he could cradle her body close to his. She tucked her head into the curve between his shoulder and neck and he felt her touch a kiss to his skin. After a few moments, Maxim pulled the blankets up higher over them, surrounding them in soothing warmth. Ivy was already falling asleep, but Maxim lay awake for several minutes longer. His hand trailed down her chest and settled on the swell of her belly. He ran his thumb along it, feeling a sense of awe come over him. When she hadn't yet told him about her pregnancy, he hadn't noticed anything different about her. Now that he knew, though, the difference was beautifully blatant. Though small, her belly was evident to him and it was as though he could sense the baby within it. It worried him that neither of them knew how this pregnancy was going to progress. Much like Eden and Pyra, this baby was unlike any that he had ever seen born. He didn't know if she would carry more like a human or more like a Mikana, which meant he couldn't predict when the baby might be born.

Cupping his hand on the side of her waist, Maxim eased Ivy's head off his shoulder and onto the pillow so that he could bring his lips to her belly. He kissed it tenderly and then turned to rest his ear against it. As he listened to the quiet sounds of her body, Maxim thought of his father. For so many years he had thought that Aegeus was dead and part of him had felt almost angered that he had allowed himself to be taken away from his sons. Now that he knew that his father was alive, however, it only confirmed what he was feeling toward the tiny child growing within his mate. He knew that there was nothing that would make him leave this child, and it would take everything to force him. He needed to see his father again and to be there when his own baby was born. He would survive whatever was to come, no matter what that took.

Maxim remembered what Elon had said about Nylek, and realized that it was the same for the rest of them. There were challenges ahead and they needed to prepare to fight, but first they needed to get through the night.

13

Sleep was brief and fitful for Pyra. He would allow himself to rest only for a few moments before he would suddenly wake so that he could check on Eden and their child tucked in her arms as she slept. Finally, some of the others around him began to shift and stir, and he knew that it was time to get moving. They had gotten a chance to refresh, but now they needed to forge ahead. As long as they were in the laboratory building, they were far more vulnerable to Ryan and his hybrids. Even though he knew that there were more waiting on Penthos for them, at least when they were there, they weren't trapped in a maze at the mercy of whatever was around the next corner. When they made it back to Penthos, they could fight.

The group was slowly pulling itself together and preparing to move on when the building around them shook and somewhere above them Pyra heard a tremendous blast. Eden sat up and scooped Lysander to her chest.

"What was that?" she asked frantically.

"I don't know, but we need to hurry," Pyra said. "Get

Lysander changed and gather anything that's here that you might be able to use. We need to move."

Pyra went around the room urging the group to prepare themselves. Soon they were gathered at the door to the emergency chamber looking to him for instructions.

"No hospital, not even one from a century ago, has only one stairwell," he said. "We followed the one on the same side of the building to get down here. Maybe if we find another one, we'll find a way out."

"Why don't we come back the way we came?" Ty asked.

"It's too dangerous," Pyra said. "We can't retrace our steps."

Pyra opened the door to the chamber cautiously, but the rest of the subterranean floor was still as silent as it had been when they found it. Several of the members of the group took out their lightsticks, while others used lanterns they had found in the emergency chamber to light their way. There seemed to be little on this floor of the hospital except for storage, and they soon made their way to the opposite side from the one where they had arrived. Here Pyra found a pale wooden door featuring a plaque with a jagged line etched onto it. He had come to recognize that symbol as representing stairs. Like the other stairwell doors that they had encountered, this one was unlocked and he stepped right through it, but paused when he noticed that there were stairs both leading up and down.

"What is it, Pyra?" Eden asked as she came into the stairwell with him.

"There are stairs leading down," he said.

"I thought that we were on the bottom floor," she said.

"I thought we were," Pyra said. "The stairs that we used to get down here didn't lead any further down."

"So, what's down there?" she asked.

"I don't know," Pyra said, "but I don't think going down is going to be the way that we get out. We should move back up into the new building and find the main exit."

They had moved up the first flight of stairs when Pyra heard a faint pounding on the wall. They all paused and Pyra listened more intently. The pounding came again and this time he thought he heard voices. Straining to hear them again, Pyra ran in the direction where he thought the pounding originated. He heard it again and this time the voices were stronger and more distinct. They were muffled by having to move through the walls of the contemporary building and the medical ward, but they were definitely voices.

Pyra!

Eden grabbed his arm.

"Did you hear that?" she asked.

Pyra nodded. One of the voices had called his name. They continued moving up the stairs and the pounding continued, seeming to grow louder the further they moved toward the main building. Pyra rushed up to the wall at the next landing and pounded his hands against it. He shouted, yelling anything to get the attention of whoever had called his name. For a brief moment he considered that it might be the hybrids taunting them and trying to lure them out, but he pushed the thought aside. Ryan hadn't bred them to be clever, he had bred them to destroy. It was far more likely that whoever was pounding on the wall was calling to him specifically, and if they were being that loud, they might not understand the danger that they were facing. He needed to get to them.

There was a beat of silence after he stopped yelling and then the pounding on the wall resumed. Pyra responded to it as he traveled up the next set of stairs trying to find it.

Suddenly it seemed that they had met. The voice cried out to him again and he heard it distinctly, the tone clear and firm. It sounded like Zuri.

"Gyyx, Ero, Ty," he called down the steps toward the men, "have you connected with your mates?"

"No," Gyyx responded as he approached. "I closed off communications with her right after we left. I didn't know what we were going to face here, and I didn't want her to sense any of it."

"Connect with her now," Pyra commanded. "All of you. Reach out to your mates. Find out where they are."

The three men each turned slightly away as they focused in on connecting their thoughts with their mates. If it was Zuri that he heard calling to him, Ero would be able to connect with her and confirm that the women were there. If it was a hybrid somehow mimicking her voice to get his attention, she would tell Ero that they were still at the house.

"It's me, Pyra," Zuri's voice shouted through the wall.

"It's her," Ero confirmed. "They're all here. They came to find us."

"They don't know about the hybrids," Pyra said. "They don't know that they're in danger."

"They must be in one of the closets," Eden said. "If they break through the wall, we'll all be able to get out."

"Tell them," Pyra said to the men. "Tell them to pick up the heaviest things that they can find and smash into the wall where they can hear my voice."

A few seconds later there was a dull crashing sound and then another. Soon the wall ahead of him looked like it was starting to crumble.

"Step back," Pyra shouted.

He waited a moment and then kicked at the weakened

section of the wall. It splintered beneath his foot and a large piece gave way. As it crumbled to the ground he could see through the resulting gap to the women and just beyond them, standing like a figment of his imagination in the shadows, was Jem.

The others standing with the women barely registered to Pyra as he scrambled through the broken wall toward the brother he thought he had lost. Jem laughed as they embraced and he held the younger warrior tightly to him. He pulled back and grasped Jem's face in his hands, holding his head still so that he could look at him. Some of the carefree softness that his face had once held was gone and he looked older, more weathered than when he had disappeared from that tree limb. As he stared at him longer, he realized that his eyes were now orange, the sign that he had found his mate.

"How are you here?" he asked. "Have you been here the whole time?"

"I'll explain everything," Jem said, "but not right now. Why are you here?"

The question broke Pyra out of the joy that he had felt at seeing Jem alive, and reminded him of the danger that they were all still in.

"Ryan captured Zsilvia and her mate George, then kidnapped Lysander. When we came here to free them he told us that he has been breeding hybrids to use as weapons."

"Hybrids?" Jem asked

"Yes," Pyra said. "He's been breeding and splicing together different species to try to create the ultimate military race so that he can take over the Universe, and he's starting with us. There are others on another planet, a planet called Penthos, and Ryan has sent some of his hybrid army there to eliminate them. The others are here, in the laboratory. We have to get past them or we won't survive."

"How many of you are here?" Jem asked.

Pyra stepped out of the way and allowed the rest of the group to stream out of the wall. He could see Jem's eyes widen as he saw Azrael and Ariella. Suddenly his expression grew dark and his hand moved to his hip the way that it had when they fought in battle.

"Get back," Jem commanded.

Pyra looked toward the wall and saw Aegeus climbing through. He held up an arm to block Jem from running toward him.

"No," Pyra said. "He's one of us. He's an ally."

"That is a Klimnu!" Jem growled.

"I know," Pyra said. "His name is Aegeus. He's been held captive by Ryan for years. He wasn't always this way. Ryan forced him to become Klimnu. He is our friend, Jem."

They heard a crash from behind Jem, followed by another, and then another. Pyra realized that all the doors along the hallway were opening and as they did, shrouded creatures stepped out of them. Pyra stiffened. Without looking away from the creatures, he tilted his head toward Eden.

"Go back down the stairwell," he said. "Get into the emergency chamber with the others and shut the door. Don't open it until you hear my voice." She hesitated and he pressed her backwards. "Go!"

14

Eden scrambled backwards through the broken wall into the stairwell again. She ran with Ariella, Elianna, and Zsilvia until they made it back to the emergency chamber. She turned and waited for Zuri, Samira, and Leia to come, and was surprised to see two other women along with them. One she recognized as Samira's mother, but the other she didn't know. They came into the room and Eden closed the door behind them.

She tried not to think of what was happening above them. She struggled to keep her mind away from the number of hybrids that could be swarming the building and whether the men would be able to fight them off. To distract herself, she turned to the unknown woman.

"Hello," she said. "I'm Eden."

The woman gave a tremulous smile.

"Jem has told me about you," she said. "I'm Angela."

"You're Jem's mate," Eden said.

Angela nodded. There were tears starting to build in her eyes and it was evident that she was overwhelmed by what was happening. Whatever she thought she was getting herself into when she came here with Jem, this was far more and she didn't know how to handle it. Suddenly Eden went from wanting to distract herself from the fear that she was feeling, to wanting to protect and surround this woman. She stepped up beside her and wrapped an arm around her shoulders.

"Come here," she said.

She guided Angela over to the side of the room where they had slept the night before and lowered her down to the makeshift bed. Zuri had found two more lanterns and hung them from the wall, providing enough light to help them see around them. Eden searched the nearby shelf of emergency rations and found coffee. She twisted the container to activate the automatic heating mechanism inside and handed it to Angela.

"Drink this," she said.

Angela held the container up to her nose and drew in a breath. Her shoulders relaxed as she filled her lungs with the rich aroma of the coffee. She took a sip and Eden heard the soft groan of someone who hadn't tasted coffee in quite some time.

"Where are you from, Angela?" Eden asked carefully.

She didn't want to push her overwrought emotions even further, but she couldn't deny her curiosity. She needed to understand what happened to Jem.

"Earth," Angela told her. She took another sip of the coffee and then shook her head. "Originally, anyway."

"Me, too," Eden said. "But you haven't been on Earth in a while, have you?"

Angela shook her head again.

"No," she said. "It's been five years since I've spent any time here."

"So, you didn't meet Jem on Earth?"

"No," Angela said.

She was starting to sound irritated and Eden settled down onto the floor beside her.

"I'm sorry," Eden said. "I don't mean to bombard you with questions. It's just...you've got to understand. We thought Jem was dead. We haven't heard anything from him since that day. He just..."

"I know," Angela said, cutting Eden off.

It wasn't a rude or aggressive gesture. Instead it felt like a desperate one, as if she couldn't bear the thought of hearing about Jem's disappearance. It was clear that she had heard the story before and it was painful to think of it again. Eden could understand. The story was only a reminder of how close Angela had come to never meeting Jem. Eden would never have wanted to think about it if Pyra had ever faced something like that.

"But where..." Zuri asked carefully, not finishing the thought as if she wanted to give Angela as much space as she could.

Angela took a final sip of coffee and rested the container on her lap. She took a breath and looked around at the women.

"Do any of you know about the HM-1313 wall?" she asked.

The women shook their heads. Angela looked down at the container in her lap and nodded. The expression on her face was pained.

"I've already been forgotten," she murmured.

"The excavation," Valerie said from behind them. She stepped up closer to the rest of the women and crouched down to look at Angela. "I remember watching about it on the news. It was a few years back. There was a research team that went into the desert across the country to do an excavation."

"Right," Angela said. "And a few of the researchers left from that project and joined other excavations around the world."

"I think I remember hearing about that," Eden said. "It seemed really strange to me that some of the team would get reassigned right in the field and wouldn't even get a chance to come back and debrief."

Angela nodded.

"That's because it is strange. Something like that would never happen, but because the investors and heads of the excavation presented a united front about it and had all the answers to all the questions, people just believed it. They went along with it rather than realizing how ridiculous that really was and demanding to find out the truth."

"What is the truth?" Valerie asked.

"We didn't go to another excavation. We went to another world."

"What do you mean?" Eden asked.

"Exactly what I said. We stepped into a cavern to explore it and in the next moment we were on a desolate, frozen planet."

"You went through a portal," Eden said in surprise.

"Yes," Angela said. "There were five of us when we went. Jacob and I are the only ones who stayed together. We haven't seen the others since just a short time after we arrived."

"Why didn't you come back?" Leia asked.

"We didn't know what had happened," Angela said. "We had no idea that we went through a portal or how to go back. It is not so simple as to just move through the same portal to go back and forth. The portal in the cavern brought us to another cavern on the frozen planet. That portal didn't connect directly back to Earth, though. The portals cross different locations and different times. When we finally found our way back to the frozen planet where we started, we stayed. It was difficult, but it was what we knew."

"How did you find Jem?" Eden asked.

"Others found us first. Galadriel and Vyker. They were traveling the streams and they found Jacob and me. They offered to bring us along with them, possibly even getting us back to Earth. We went with them, but we lost them along the way. They found another planet and Jem was there. He traveled back with them and discovered that he had a portal that brought them back to Earth. From there, they made it back to the original stream and to Vyker. That's when I met Jem. After that we figured out the path that connected Vyker and Galadriel's planet and the one where Jem had been living. His planet was so beautiful. Warm and untouched. I chose to go live there with him."

Angela was breathless when she finished and Eden felt the same way. It was a complex and overpowering story, difficult to even fathom, but she knew that Angela was telling her the truth. Jem's reappearance proved that there was so much that Eden didn't understand, so much that was still unknown about the world.

"We're very happy that you're here now," Eden said. "Both of you."

Angela tried to offer a smile, but the tears had built in her eyes again. She hung her head and ran one of her fingertips along the rim of the container of coffee in her lap.

"We were just trying to get back to Uoria," she said weakly. "Jem wanted to get home, even for a time. When we got here, we found Rilex and he told us that there were problems on Uoria."

Eden felt a heaviness in her chest. She nodded. She wished that she could explain everything to Angela, but there was just too much. For now, she was going to have to trust in them. As Jem's mate, she was bound to him for life. It would be her decision if she would follow that bond and stay with Jem or if she would turn her back on him. Knowing her own devotion to Pyra and the unbreakable tie that she felt to him, she knew how unlikely it would be that Angela would be able to walk away from her mate. She was one of them now, part of this, another piece of the resistance they were building against an enemy that was seeming larger and more oppressive with each passing moment.

"What's happening up there?" Angela asked.

Eden lifted her eyes to the ceiling of the emergency chamber.

"The hybrid army," Eden said. "The men are fighting them. We have to get through them before we can get out of the lab and back to our vehicles to travel to the others."

Angela's eyes suddenly went clear.

"Why are we sitting here?" she asked. "If they are up there fighting, why are we down here?"

"Pyra told us to stay here until he came for us."

"And we are all just supposed to listen to him?"

"He's Eden's mate and the leader of the Denynso warriors, which makes him the leader for the rest of us."

Angela set the container to the side and stood.

"He's neither to me," she said.

She stalked to a shelf along the wall and took up a long metal pole with a sharpened blade on the end. Eden watched her cross to the door.

"What are you doing?" Eden asked.

"I survived for five years with nothing. I came up against creatures that I had never seen and conditions that seemed completely insurmountable, but I survived. I didn't do that by hiding. I don't know what's up there, but I do know that I'm not going to let Jem face it alone. If there is someone who is trying to take over the Universe, I'm not just going to let it happen. He's going to have to get through my mate, and he's going to have to get through me."

Angela's words reawakened the fire that had burned within Eden. She had fought alongside the Denynso before. She had stood up and refused to give Ryan the satisfaction of knowing that he was still controlling her, that he was succeeding in the plan that he had manipulated her into being a part of long before she even left Earth for Uoria. Now she had been weakened and broken down, and instead of reaching within her to find the Denynso that dwelled there and letting it power her through as it had when she faced off against Ryan in the lab, she had hidden. Not anymore. She stood and nodded.

"She's right," Eden said. "What happened to us? Why are we here with our men? Because we fought to be here. We stood by their sides and fought to get here, and I'm not going to stop fighting. Ryan started this with me, and I'm going to be a part of ending it. I don't know where he is right now. For all I know he could be watching every move, delighting in us running through this place like mice and hiding from the creatures that he designed for this very purpose. He wants Pyra's blood. He wants to be able to take out the Denynso and turn all of us and all of our allies into slaves to help him conquer the Universe. I am not going to just let that happen."

"What about Lysander?" Valerie asked.

Eden leaned down and touched a kiss to her son's head.

"Lysander *is* Pyra's blood. He has the soul of a Denynso warrior. He was born for battle. When he's grown and has taken his father's place as the leader, he will know that he is the strongest and most powerful Denynso warrior that has ever been because he was conceived against adversity, carried through battle, born into conflict, and raised in war. He will never back down." She used a blanket to tighten the sling around the baby, crossing it over like armor. "And neither will I." '

A few minutes later the women marched up the stairs, each bearing a weapon they had scavenged from the emergency chambers. They could hear the grunts and crashes of the conflict going on above them and the sounds fueled them forward. The door to the closet concealing the sealed stairwell had been closed, but Eden forced it open. The corridor that stretched in front of her was strewn with bodies, the walls splattered with blood. The rest of the space was filled with figures tangled in combat and Eden scanned them to find Pyra. When she did, her heart steeled even further and she lifted the sharpened blade above her head.

The women streamed into the corridor and instantly Eden's mind was clouded by the compulsion for battle given to her by the Denynso DNA now in her cells. She clashed against the impending enemies with everything in her, using her incredible strength and the skills that she had learned from watching her mate. She fought nearly blindly, keeping her back to those that she fought against to protect Lysander from their weapons. Around her she could see the others engaged in their own battles against the tremendous array of hybrids that confronted them. Some fought independently against the smaller creatures, while others teamed up against the larger ones. Blood streaked against their skin and clothes hung in tatters, but they kept going.

The sound of the battle began to lessen as more of the hybrids lay dead or dying at their feet. Soon the intensity with which it had raged reduced to an ember. Eden had reached the end of the hallway and leaned against the wall in front of her, catching her breath. She turned slowly to survey the carnage scattered on the floor, praying that she would see all of their group standing. As she let her eyes travel across the shadowy hallway she saw some of their number crouched or lying across the marble. Jem was sitting leaned against the wall, his large hand clutched against his chest. His breathing was ragged and his eyes were closed.

Eden rushed to Jem's side and dropped down beside him.

"Jem," she said. "Jem, open your eyes. Ciyrs!" She shouted for the healer, then looked for Angela. Their eyes met and Angela ran over. "Jem, Angela's here."

Jem's eyes opened enough that he could see his mate kneeling beside him and then closed them again. Ciyrs came to him and touched his hand to Jem's chest above the warrior's hand.

"Jem, is this the only place you're injured?" the healer asked.

Jem nodded.

"Yes," he said. "Glass."

Eden looked up at the tremendous window that stretched across the front of the administrative offices and saw that it was shattered. One of the hybrids must have used Valdician powers to throw Jem into the glass, splintering it. Ciyrs took Jem's hand and carefully moved it aside. Eden could see a large shard of glass protruding from the wound in Jem's chest. Her hand flew to her mouth and she closed her eyes briefly.

"Alright, Jem," Ciyrs said. "We're going to get that out

and I'm going to fix you up. We already lost you once. We're not doing it again."

Jem managed a meager smile and weak laugh as he shook his head.

"I'm not going anywhere," he said. "Dying once was enough for me for now."

Ciyrs stood and called out to Pyra.

"We need to get Jem down to the medical ward," he said. "There isn't time to try to get him to the shuttle. I need to get that glass out of him and start the healing right now. I'll check the others here and bring down anyone else who will need healing. We're going to have to spend at least the night here."

The idea of spending another night in the laboratory sent a chill through Eden. She had spent enough time there when she was on Earth. She wanted to put it behind her and never think of its corridors and doorways again. If they were going to be strong enough when they made it to Penthos and the others, however, she knew that the warriors would need their injuries healed. For now, the hybrid forces had been pushed back and it didn't seem that more were on their way. They could spend some time recuperating and then escape to the shuttle bay and head to Penthos the next morning. As the group began to make their way back through the closet wall and down the stairs, Eden evaluated the bodies lying on the ground. If they did return, she was confident they'd be ready.

She waited as those who made it through the battle uninjured helped the wounded out of the corridor and down into the abandoned medical unit. It seemed Jem was the most grievously injured. When only Zuri, Ariella, and Jacob were left in the corridor, she headed toward the door. She was nearly at the closet when she felt a hand clasp around her ankle. Eden gasped and clutched Lysander closer to her chest as she tried to pull out of the hybrid's grip.

"Please."

The voice was weak and raspy, startling Eden enough to make her look down to whatever had her in its grip. The hood of the creature lying on the ground beneath her had fallen away, revealing a bloodied face and close-shorn black hair. Beneath the veil of oil-like blood along one side of its face she saw what looked like a tattoo etched into its skin.

"Please," the creature said again. "Downstairs. Help them. Please. Help them."

15

Maxim walked through the main chamber of the shuttle in the faint early morning light, trying to keep as quiet as he could as he made his way toward the infirmary. The others had only laid down to sleep a couple of hours before, but he had been unable to rest more than an hour after feeling Ivy fall tenderly to sleep in his arms. There was so much on his mind that it wouldn't let his body rest. He didn't want his movements to wake Ivy, so he climbed carefully out of bed, dressed, and started toward the infirmary to check on Kyven.

"Good morning, Maxim."

Elise's voice in the hazy corridor between the main chamber and the kitchen startled Maxim and he whipped around to see her standing in the kitchen stirring something in a tall cup. She was fully dressed and looked as polished as she did when they first entered the shuttle, telling him that she hadn't been able to sleep well, either.

"Good morning," he said. "Is everything alright?"

She let out a sigh and shook her head.

"I still haven't been able to communicate with Azra," she said. "I haven't heard from him since we first got redirected to Uoria. I'm really worried about him. What do you think they're doing? Why hasn't he communicated with me?"

"Have you tried to communicate with him?" Maxim asked.

Elise looked down into the cup that she was stirring as if whatever as inside was going to give her the answers to all her concerns.

"Yes," she said. "Many times. He just isn't responding. I didn't even know that I had the ability to communicate with him like this, but now that I can't I feel panicked all the time."

"I'm sure that there's a reason he isn't communicating with you," Maxim said. "He needs all of his concentration and focus right now. You heard Ryan just as well as I did. What we're going through here isn't the end of it. He drew the others to him there and has them at his mercy. The Denynso wouldn't just allow that to happen, though. They are fighting and they will continue to fight."

"What am I supposed to do?" Elise asked. "Am I supposed to just sit around here and wait for him to show up or to find out that he's dead? How do I even keep going? What am I supposed to do if he dies?"

"You can't think about that," Maxim said. "You can't worry about him. He is a Denynso warrior. This is what he is made for, Elise. It is his life. Now that you are his mate, it is your life, too. What you do now is honor him by being courageous and giving yourself to the same cause that he has given himself to."

"How do I do that? I can't fight. I've never seen anything like what's going on here. I've spent my whole life sheltered, and then when I started my career I thought that I was choosing something that would be adventurous. I wanted to see more and explore the galaxy and other planets. What I didn't know is that I was still completely sheltered. I wasn't seeing reality. I was seeing what these planets and travel companies constructed for their customers to see. Then I met Azra and everything changed. Suddenly it was like my world expanded. It had been watercolors and pastels and then it was vibrant and full. It wasn't until all of this happened, though, that I realized just how much everything had really changed. I'm never going to be able to go back. I've seen it. I've witnessed this and I know, at least partially, what's happening, and I can't pretend that it didn't happen or that it isn't out there. My life won't ever be the same."

"Of course it won't," Maxim said. "My life isn't the same since I met Ivy. The moment that I found her, everything was different, and I wouldn't change it for a single second. Even though we've struggled and had to face things that I never would have imagined, knowing what I do now, I would never go back to the life that I had before the Denynso came into the kingdom and brought us back to the Earth settlement. Even more, I know that I never would have been able to do any of this without Ivy. What you are going through is hard, and I promise you that it is only going to get harder. You're a part of this now, though. From the moment that you met Azra and realized that you were his mate, you became a part of something so much larger than you can imagine. Probably much larger than any of us can imagine, even those of us who have been in it since the beginning."

"Aren't you scared?" Elise asked.

"Yes," Maxim admitted. "But there are things worth being scared for. Even if I don't live through this, what I've done is worth it."

"Why?"

Her voice was quiet and strained, as if she was reaching out to him desperately, needing for him to tell her something that would make what she was facing make sense and reassure her. She looked smaller and more frightened than she had the day before. It was as if she had been filled with adrenaline and anger when she confronted the crew that had abandoned her, but now it had all drained away and only left the uncertainty. He took another step closer to her so that she could better see his eyes in the glow of the sun that was rising behind him.

"Because this moment and this world aren't yours alone. If you pretend that they are and keep your eyes covered to what's going on around you, you are just existing. To live is to honor the past, serve the present, and craft the future for yourself, for those who have already come, and for those yet to arrive. Even if I had to give up my life for it, it would be worth it, knowing that I didn't just sit by and allow Ryan to disrespect the past and try to steal the future."

"This is really happening, isn't it, Maxim?" she asked.

Maxim nodded.

"It is. There's nothing that you can do to stop it. All you can do is look inside yourself, find the strength, and hang on."

Elise held the tall cup out to Maxim.

"This is for Kyven," she said. "You can bring it to him."

"He's awake?" Maxim asked, feeling a boost of hope.

Elise nodded.

"I checked on him when I first woke up. It seems like the healing has really set in. You can go ahead and see him."

Maxim took the cup from her hand and rushed toward the infirmary. He stepped inside and saw Emerie sitting on the side of Kyven's bed, her hands pressed to his chest. Kyven looked over at her and a smile crossed his face.

"Kyven," Maxim said. "Are you alright?"

"I'm getting there," he said.

Emerie nodded and took her hands away.

"He is," Emerie said. "He should probably rest a little longer, but the healing ointments worked. The effects of the toxins have ended and his wounds are mending well. The sutures haven't been rejected and I don't see any signs of infection."

Maxim walked to the edge of the bed and offered Kyven the cup.

"Elise said that this is for you," he said.

"Drink all of it," Elise said, stepping into the room. "It will help keep infection at bay."

Kyven took a swing from the cup and Maxim saw his face clench and contort. He made a gagging sound and pulled the cup away from him as fast as he could, holding it out to Elise. She glanced down into it and shook her head.

"What?" he choked out.

"All of it," Elise said. Maxim saw Kyven clench his lips and shake his head. "*All* of it."

Maxim laughed as Kyven let out a groan like she was asking him to undergo torture and pulled the cup back so that he could swallow down the rest of the cup's contents. Kyven coughed as he pushed the cup insistently back toward Elise.

"What was that?" Maxim asked.

"Medicine," Elise said. "It's part of the supplies that Elon brought with us."

"That stuff might be worse than the toxin," Kyven said, his face still contorted. "I don't understand how you humans handle it."

Maxim laughed again. The happiness that he felt from seeing his brother back to himself was indescribable. He felt strengthened and revived, ready to face whatever the day was going to bring. Suddenly he remembered Nylek. He turned and looked at the bed across the room. Nylek was still lying still, his eyes closed. Elon was standing beside him evaluating the lines and symbols appearing on a screen above his head.

"How is he?" Maxim asked.

Elon looked up at him and the strained look in his eyes told Maxim that he hadn't slept much the night before, if at all. If he was anything like Ciyrs, Elon was too committed to watching over the patients that he was trying to help to think about himself. The thought was reassuring, but Maxim had to admit that the methods Elon was using were intimidating. The doctors in his own kingdom were far more like Ciyrs, though even the Denynso healer had more complex and advanced healing techniques than the Mikana. All of the machinery and medicines seemed to put a separation between Elon and the man he was trying to save, though Nylek did look stronger than he had the night before. The thought made Maxim wonder if he would ever really understand the humans and if Ivy ever felt the same way about him and the Mikana.

"He's showing improvement," Elon said. "Whatever got to him last night did some pretty serious internal damage and he was nearly frozen. I'm trying to stabilize his body temperature and regulate his vitals before I attempt surgery to repair the damage."

"Surgery?" Maxim demanded, standing up from Kyven's side and stalking across the Elon. "You didn't ask if you could perform internal surgery."

"I didn't know that I needed to," Elon said. "This is my

infirmary. You are passengers on my ship and when medical decisions need to be made, I will make them."

"We are not your passengers," Maxim said. "We're hostages. As we've already established with Avery, you have no power over us."

"Nylek is Denynso," Maxim said. "If he needs further healing, he should be given the healing that he is accustomed to. The healing of his kind. Ciyrs trained both Lynx and me to use the ointments and herbs that we packed to handle injuries."

"This man is severely injured," Elon argued. "I need to perform surgery to see the full extent of the damage and repair it effectively. I have access to advanced medical technology that will make it safer and easier, and give him a chance to survive."

"He doesn't need medical technology," Maxim said, offended by the man's words. "Ciyrs has been healing his kind since he was barely out of childhood. The herbs and ointments that he sent with us are powerful enough to handle virtually anything that we might encounter."

"There's a reason that humans once only used herbs to handle their medical needs and then progressed past it."

"That'll be enough, Elon," Avery said as he stepped into the infirmary. "I won't have you disrespecting them."

"It's not a matter of disrespect," Elon said. "It's facts. It's reality. Their healer isn't even here, but I've seen this man do what he passes as medical care. All the other Denynso did was clean his wounds and apply ointments."

"It worked, didn't it?" Avery pointed out. "Kyven is awake and regaining his strength by the minute."

"Because he's been taking strong doses of medication and I stitched his wounds. This is different. Nylek was seriously injured out there and we don't know how. Unless we know what is happening inside his body, doing anything else could cause him far more harm than good. I know that man feels that he knows best and that he taught the others how to do things well enough to handle these situations, but we both know that that's not the case."

"That man's name is Ciyrs," Maxim said, "and he is a Denynso healer. Humans developed tools and technology because the entirety of the understanding of herbs and plants for medical care doesn't even begin to compare to what only Ciyrs has. What he does is far more than just putting his hands on them. The powers and capabilities that this man has are unfathomable to you."

Maxim felt like his chest was going to burst with the anger that was causing his heart to pound heavily against his ribs. How dare this man question Ciyrs and his abilities? How dare he imply that because he had machines and complex medications, he was automatically better than the born healer who had been saving the lives of his entire clan for nearly his entire life?

"How do you know?" Elon asked. "You aren't even Denynso."

"No," Maxim said, shaking his head, "I'm not. You're right about that. But I was nearly Klimnu."

"What's that?" Elon asked.

"Something more horrible than I can begin to tell you. I would have suffered more than you can ever understand. The only reason that that didn't happen to me was because of Ciyrs. He kept me as I am. He has saved countless lives, including that of his own mate, who nearly died at the hands of their enemies but was brought back from the brink by his care. We weren't born to heal the way he was and the only tools that we have might be the herbs and ointments that he sent along with us, but I trust that that's enough.

Even if it isn't, you have no place questioning it just because we aren't human."

Elon looked stung and he stepped back slightly. It was clear he didn't know what to say. Avery stepped forward and reached a beseeching hand toward Maxim.

"I'm sorry, Maxim," he said. "I promised to help you and reassured you that my crew was here for you. I've already failed at that."

Maxim shook his head.

"You didn't fail," he said. "I still appreciate the assistance you've offered."

A groan from Nylek's bed broke the tension that had built among the men. Maxim looked down and saw the warrior's head moving slowly back and forth. He didn't open his eyes, but his lips parted and he let out a breath before speaking.

"Mhavyrch," he murmured.

Maxim heard Kyven gasp behind him and he turned to look at Kyven.

"What did he just say?" Kyven asked. "Did he just say Mhavyrch?"

Maxim nodded, confused by the word that had come from the apparently still unconscious warrior's lips.

"Yes," he said. "Mhavyrch. Miracle. How does he know an ancient Mikana word?"

Kyven shook his head.

"No," he said, sounding excited. "No, it's not a word. It's a name. It's a person."

"A person?" Maxim asked.

"Mhavyrch," Emerie whispered. "How does he know?"

"A person?" Maxim asked again. "How does he know what?"

Maxim hated the feeling of confusion that was rushing

over him. It felt like he was missing something, like there was a piece that he somehow overlooked so he wasn't able to keep up with the conversation that was unraveling around him.

"We weren't alone in the quarry," Kyven explained. "When we fell through the rocks into the cavern, it was just Emerie and me. Our lightstick was fading and we could hear the creature coming. The Meldor."

"Meldor?" Avery repeated.

Kyven nodded.

"The less light there was, the closer it got. When our light went out, I was sure that we were going to die. I did everything that I could to protect Emerie, but I couldn't see what was in that chamber with us, so I couldn't fight. It attacked me, but before it could kill me, there was suddenly light."

Kyven seemed out of breath and Maxim walked back to the side of his bed so that he could guide his brother back to lie down.

"You need to rest," he said. "Emerie, can you tell us what happened?"

She nodded as she reached for Kyven's hand.

"The light was blinding, but it was the most wonderful light that I had ever seen. A man had come down into the cavern with us and brought a ball of light that pushed the creature back. He told us that it was called a Meldor and that few who ever encounter it live. Before he left he told us that his name was Mhavyrch."

"Why didn't you tell us this?" Maxim asked.

"He was gone by the time that you got there to help us. I didn't know if I should tell you."

"Why?" Maxim asked. "He helped you. He saved your life."

"He was a hybrid."

The words struck Maxim silent. In the stillness that fell over the infirmary they heard footsteps rushing toward them. Lila appeared at the doorway with a look of fear in her eyes.

"What is it, Lila?" Elise asked.

The woman shook her head as if she couldn't speak and gestured for them to follow her. Maxim looked at his brother again, and then ran out of the room and down the hallway toward the main chamber. He was partway there when he heard the low rhythm of drums in the distance. It was a slow, steady beat, like one that would correspond with a controlled march. The sound seemed to hold more resonance than its volume justified and Maxim felt like it was pricking at his skin.

He got to the main chamber and saw that the sun had finally made its way all the way up. It glowed through the window on the far wall and splashed like gold across the floor and furniture throughout the room. It should have been soothing. It should have invigorating to finally see the sun again, as dark as the sun on Penthos might be, but it didn't represent the newness and possibility that a fresh day should. Instead, it was exposure, forcing them to see the planet where they had been dropped into Ryan's disturbing game and what was waiting for them there.

The sound of the drums continued, seeming to get louder. He rushed to the window and looked out, but he didn't see anything except the never-ending expanse of sand that stretched around the desert.

"What is it, Maxim?" Elise asked as she came into the room.

"I don't know," he said.

He ran through the pod chambers to the room that he

shared with Ivy. She was sitting up in the bed, looking around with wide, confused eyes.

"Do you hear that?" she asked. "What is it?"

Maxim shook his head. He pressed a button on the wall across from the bed and watched as the flat panels that covered the window slid open. He pressed his hands against it and looked out, trying to see if there was something more out there that wasn't visible from the window in the main chamber. Not seeing anything else but the shimmering sand did nothing to comfort him. If anything, it only made the fear that was beginning to prick the back of his neck more intense. He could feel the rhythm of the drums in his blood and the threat that they carried in a chill that rolled down his spine.

"Get dressed," he told Ivy. "I don't want you to leave the shuttle, but I want you to be ready."

"Ready for what?" she asked as she stood from the bed.

She was still undressed from him gently pulling away her nightgown the night before, and her beautiful bare body in the morning sunlight underscored the vulnerability that was setting in. Maxim stepped up to her and wrapped an arm around her waist so that he could sweep her up against his body and crush his mouth down on hers. He kissed her with all of the intensity that he was feeling, the desperation to keep her close, and the brutal, primal energy that was building within him with each beat of the drum outside. She sought him in that kiss, connecting with him and reassuring him with her sweetness and familiarity, but also with the promise of loyalty that she had given him when they were still on Uoria.

When their lips parted, Maxim crossed to the luggage pod on the opposite side of the chamber and lifted its lid. He withdrew the weapons that he had brought along with him and the supply bag that he had packed before leaving Uoria. Maxim loaded his body with the weapons, ensuring each was easily accessible so that he would be able to grab and use them however and whenever they were needed. He picked up his cloak and looked down at it in his hands. Now that the morning sun had come to burn away the chill from the night before he didn't know if he needed the cloak, but he still swung it around his shoulders and tightened it around his neck. He pulled the cloth around his body, concealing all of the weapons and providing a slight layer of additional protection.

Maxim walked back to the bed and leaned down to lift Ivy's nightgown off the floor. He took the pale blue silk ribbon around the neckline in his fingertips and eased it out of the gauzy fabric, using it to tie his hair at the back of his neck. Feeling fully prepared, he turned back to the window and closed the panels again to conceal the inside of the chamber again. He stepped up to Ivy and touched his hand to her cheek.

"Stay in the shuttle," he said again. "Stay with the other women and wait for me to come back."

"I'm not just going to sit around here, Maxim."

Maxim touched a kiss to the center of her forehead.

"I love you," he said.

He took a moment to touch his fingertips to her belly and then rushed out of the room. The sound of the drums was louder now. He could feel each beat shaking through the air around him. He knew what it was. He had heard of it before. When he made it back to the main chamber he saw Rain standing at the window, her arms wrapped around her body. The panels were only open a few inches but she was staring intently through them. She turned to him as Maxim stepped into the room with Zyyr and Lynx close behind him. Her eyes met his as if she could transfer the images that she had just gathered into him with only that look. There was a long, tense moment with only the sound of the heavy, pounding drums reverberating from the metal around them to accent each breath. Finally, she spoke.

"They're here."

UNTITLED

To be continued...

9 781953 126146